I0743455

For Avery

A LANDEN ACRES NOVEL

NATALIE JESS

Copyright © 2023 by Greenstone Publishing

All rights reserved.

No portion of this book may be reproduced in any form without written permission from the publisher or author, except as permitted by U.S. copyright law.

The story, all names, characters, and incidents portrayed in this production are fictitious. No identification with actual persons (living or deceased), places, buildings, and products is intended or should be inferred.

Book Cover by Storyville Design

Edits by My Notes in the Margins

Proofread by My Notes in the Margins

Interior Format by Luna Blooms PA

To my spouse – I choose you every day.

Contents

Prologue
Avery

One *Year Ago*

I can't sit in my room staring at a wrapped present all day, can I?

No. Right?

That would defeat the purpose of having the courage to maybe-sort-of-hint at what I'm too chickenshit to handle.

What's the worst that could happen? Jackson could laugh at me. Not that he ever has.

Plus, Chase wouldn't go off the deep end at his best friend's party just because I brought a present for the birthday boy.

Buck up, Avery Jo, it's not like you aren't heading back to grad school tomorrow. You're a Barnett, and if there's one thing Barnetts are known for, it's not backing down when things are tough.

With that pep talk, I walk up to the cowboy-themed wrapping paper tied with rough twine that looks like rope and grab it with confidence I'm going to have to fake.

Just don't be weird about it, I remind myself as I leave the safety of my room.

I can see him through the windows at the top of the stairs, standing in one of his less-worn flannel shirts, and a damn fine pair of jeans. He has his brown Stetson on that matches his boots. God, I'm a sucker for cowboys.

No, that's not true. I've never dated a cowboy.

I'm a sucker for Jackson Landen.

The man would make a Speedo sexy as hell, whereas anyone else I know would just look ridiculous. I shut my eyes and try to clear my brain of the visual of Jackson in a banana hammock, which is making me weak in the knees.

Letting out a sharp breath, I make sure I'm not crushing the present and put one foot in front of the other, eventually making it to the door. I let myself pause for one more moment before I walk right up to Jackson and give him his birthday present. Because this is normal. My own brother is hosting the event and his wife planned it. I've known Jackson my whole life, so there's nothing weird about this.

I open what might be the loudest screen door known to humankind, and for once, let myself follow the insistent tug I always feel that leads me to him.

Damn. Jackson's staring right at me the second I step onto the front porch. I force my feet to keep going as I walk up to him, heart thumping and a blush creeping up my chest.

I'm rewarded with a soft smile as he says, "I thought you might have left already."

"And miss your big day? Never." I don't sound flustered, so I give myself brownie points.

He nods at the gift in my hand. "What's that?"

"What do you think, Jackson? It's your birthday party."

"You know you didn't have to get me anything," he mumbles. He looks a little shy for once.

"Don't think anything of it," I say, trying not to roll my eyes at myself as I think about how much went into the gift.

I set the present next to him with the rest of the boxes and bags waiting to be opened. He'll hate unwrapping these gifts because everyone will be watching, but he's been a good sport so far about Chase throwing such a big party.

As much as I want to stay and talk, I don't want to push my luck with being able to keep a casual demeanor around Jackson, so I allow myself to squeeze his arm. *Jesus, his muscles are amazing.* I wish him a happy birthday and walk over to where Tommy and Courtney are handling drinks and snacks just as Chase claps to get everyone's attention.

Poor Jackson is trying so hard to not let on how miserable he is. I think only Chase and Jackson's brothers know how uncomfortable he is in crowds. He typically does a good job hiding it.

But you can see his smile, which can be so sure and almost cocky, doesn't reach his eyes. He purposefully unclenches his hands. And sometimes it seems as if his mind takes him some place else. This time it's during Chase's speech, when he's talking about the day Jackson brought Misty home to Landen Acres and Chase kept her calm with boxes of sugar cubes while Jackson checked her over, Jackson does something out of character. Normally, Jackson has a snarky remark each time Chase refers to himself as Misty's "Sugar Daddy," but he keeps the same expression on his face throughout the whole story.

We all raise our drinks to toast Jackson, who holds his beer in the air, looking visibly relieved. At least for the two seconds before Chase announces it's time for the birthday boy to open his presents. Now he just looks like a deer caught in the headlights at the thought of having everyone watch him.

But he's responding to the little things people call out as he starts opening gifts one by one, and he has his usual charm back. He's playing the proper gentleman, making a brief connection with the guest who gave the gift he opens without playing favorites.

Except, I notice he avoids mine, though, and I'm trying not to read into it.

No one picks presents like they do teams, right?

Prologue
Jackson

I keep skipping Avery's present. I can feel myself blushing each time I think about reaching for, and finally opening, it.

I had to remind myself that she likely wasn't going to show up and now I have to stop myself from constantly looking her way. I almost had myself convinced that she went back to school early, which probably would have been for the best. It's not like the person I've been pining over for years would likely do more than say "happy birthday" before she'd go hang out with Tommy and Courtney. I swear, I live for those moments when she smiles or calls me by my full name. But she's *here*. And she got me something. It's sitting right next to me wrapped in paper with horses and cowboys and tied with a string or ribbon that looks like the rope we use to guide horses and lasso cattle. I risk a quick glance her way.

Jesus. She's wearing one of her sundresses and picking up a piece of wrapping paper that got away, giving me a fucking perfect view of her magnificent cleavage. Good lord, I need to get over her. Chase would kill me if he knew the things I wanted to do with her.

I suppress a moan and refocus on the next gift. I only have one more to go before hers and I unwrap what's clearly a thermos from Mrs. Fields, the newly single eighty-five-year-old who has been hinting at wanting to have a picnic by a lake.

"Thank you, Mrs. Fields. I'm sure I can think of somewhere special to take this soon." I throw her a wink, which seems to satisfy her.

I pretend to remember Avery's gift, which is literally touching my leg.

"And this one is from my best friend's baby sister." I always add the "baby" to remind myself she's one-hundred percent off-limits.

She grimaces playfully.

Focus, Jackson.

I rip through the paper, just like every gift before, even though I'd like nothing more than to take my time looking at how she wrapped it. Actually, I'd like nothing more than to tell everyone to get the hell out of here so I can lay Avery Barnett down on this patio table with her little sundress tossed to the side and her legs wrapped around my waist as I pound into her until she screams my name at least three different times.

I force myself to peek at the thermos once more to get my mind off that visual before letting something cold fall into my hand.

Inside there's a belt buckle.

It's beautiful.

I know I can't look at it very long, but it's the Landen Acres logo and she's had *Jackson Landen* engraved in the middle instead.

I look up to meet her eyes and smile.

"This is awesome! Where the heck did you get this done?" To everyone else, it probably looks like I'm being nice to my best friend's baby sister. But it feels like she saw how still I was the moment I saw the gift. Like she can sense the intensity rolling off of me that I'm burying as deep as I can while I say words that are meant to seem kind and brotherly.

"Just a random site I came across," she says with a dismissive wave and a blush creeping up her neck.

Yeah right. This buckle is clearly one of a kind. She found someone to take the Landen Acres logo and put my name in the middle instead. Not to mention the feel of the piece itself. The weight, the attention to detail, and the small indents to help the light catch just right all scream hand-crafted.

It's not until almost all the guests are gone that the buckle leaves my hand. I try to not make it obvious as I look around for her, but I don't see her outside anymore even though it's only my brothers and the Barnetts now. I know I can leave, but this is practically my second home so I hop right into dish duty.

"Absolutely not, Jax!" I hear Ava call from the kitchen doorway, hauling a folding chair back to the basement. "Avery, get that sponge out of his hands."

I hear footsteps coming up the stairs and around the corner comes Avery, ready with a what-were-you-even-thinking look on her face and a hand reaching for the sponge. Damn, she's beautiful.

"I'll give you the sponge if you let me dry."

She frowns at me. "Nothing else?"

"Nothing else, scout's honor," I reply, tentatively placing the sponge in her palm.

"You were never a scout," she mumbles, rolling her eyes.

I'll take that as a win.

She dives into scrubbing the serving dishes that won't stand a chance of fitting into the dishwasher, rinsing them with steaming water before handing them to me.

Our fingers touch, but neither of us reacts.

At least I don't think she does. I'm too busy staring at her hand that's already scrubbing a new dish with abandon.

Well, even if it doesn't mean anything to her, I can consider this my last gift from her. Just a moment of connection. And then I'll get over her. For good.

I clear my throat. "You'll have to tell me the *random* website you used for the buckle. I already know my brothers will want their own."

"I doubt I have the confirmation anymore. I did a huge clean out of my university email for all personal things." Anyone else might have believed her, but I know she's flat out lying. And that makes me way too happy.

"Well, if you did, then they can just be jealous about me having the one and only," I say, casually playing along.

Definitely the one and only.

Something pops into my head, something I feel the need to confirm. "Your brother mentioned you have a date when you head back…"

Way to keep the jealousy out of your voice, Jax.

"Um, yeah, Gary. He asked me out a few times already, and I finally gave in."

God, this is weirder than I expected. I already hate this guy. I know he isn't good enough for her. Just like the rest of her exes.

"Why'd you say no in the first place?" I ask. I don't move as I wait for her to answer, not wanting to spook her.

"Oh, I guess I didn't really have a good reason now that I think about it," she says, concentrating on scrubbing an already-clean spot on the platter. "What about you?"

"Gary didn't ask me out, so I don't need a reason to tell him no," I reply easily as she rolls her eyes, laughing.

"No, are you dating anyone?" She's still working on the same spot.

"I wouldn't call it dating," I tell her truthfully.

Well, it's part of the truth, at least. I could technically call it not-being-able-to-be-with-the-girl-I-actually-want. Being upfront with people and telling them I don't "date" keeps expectations low.

She gazes up at me with a look that's almost pity mixed with a little sadness. "Of course not. You have a reputation to uphold."

"Some might say that."

"Chase does." She passes me the platter and grabs a huge serving bowl.

"Do you believe everything your brother tells you?" I ask.

She pauses, letting out a deep breath. Her eyes lock with mine.

"No, Jackson, I don't."

"Me neither."

Chapter 1
Avery

Present Day

The phone rings over my speakerphone as I throw a handful of granola bars in my bag. Who knew defending your thesis would make you so hungry?

"Chase, pick up your damn phone for once," I say, staring accusingly at the screen.

I hear the connection happen with a bright, "Hey!"

"He does exist!"

"Unfair."

"Not at all. I usually have to go through your wife to get your attention and I'm not about to bother the woman who is literally growing my next niece or nephew."

"I mean, have you seen Ava? It's hard to keep my attention on anything else..."

"Gross. I love the girl and know how babies are made, but I don't need to be reminded that my *brother* had to do said things with her."

He just chuckles and I can picture that grin he undoubtedly has plastered on his face. "What can I do for you, sis?"

"How's my truck?" I ask, filling my water bottle.

"They're still waiting for the back-ordered piece...probably two more weeks."

"Okay, I was going to come home this weekend with a small load, but Stacy said I can borrow her car. Can you and Dad come back with me during the week to pack up the rest and haul it home? It'll work with two trucks."

"I should be able to if we can do Tuesday and Wednesday, but Dad is tied up with council meetings this week."

"Can you ask Jackson?" I keep my voice neutral, my heart fluttering.

"Why don't you ask Tommy?" He has a little edge in his tone that I know all too well.

"Because Tommy will be inspiring the next generation of math nerds."

"What?"

"He was asked to do a presentation to the senior math classes, so I know next week is out. So, it makes sense to ask your best friend. A best friend who has more flexibility on weekdays than his brothers. We'd just need him on Wednesday, and I'd bake you both oatmeal chocolate chunk cookies," I add sweetly.

"I don't know if the cookies will be enough. He's going to be a little stressed the next time I see him."

"Chase, what did you do?" I accuse.

"Nothing!"

"Chase..."

He huffs. "I just got done meeting with Sam." My jaw clenches but I don't interrupt. "She insists that he does the 'Date A Cowboy' auction."

Be normal.

"I mean, it was his idea to use the funds for new equipment to lure a large animal vet, right?" I ask.

"Yeah."

"So it makes sense that he's involved somehow, but why not have him set up the stage or something? The only thing he hates more than crowds, is being the center of attention."

"I told Sam the same thing, but she said she's already finished everything, and the campaigns already note that he'll be up for grabs. She's even sending him a shirt to wear and 'that's that,'" he says, mimicking her voice.

My hackles rise at the thought of Samantha Davies having the nerve to make Jackson be on stage in front of everyone, wearing the brand-new shirt *she* bought him. "Who is she to dress him up and tell him what to do?" I say, hoping my tone comes off annoyed-on-Jackson's-behalf and not raging-jealous.

"You clearly forgot that she was the girl who paraded him around town for a month before he ended things, per usual."

I guess I can be grateful I never had to see them together.

"It was a rhetorical question. You're aware that he's going to do what he can to get out of this, right?"

"Well, Miss I'm-finishing-my-masters-in-predicting-the-future, feel free to tell me what I can do to get him up there, so my pregnant wife doesn't have to hound his ass since she's one of the volunteers for it."

"It's an MBA in Analytics and Intelligence, jackass." And then I have an idea. It might be absolutely horrible, especially since my brother is the one who will rip it to shreds if he can, but my heart skips a beat all the same. "Tell Jackson that I'll bid on him."

Chase snorts. "Yeah right. Like I would ever allow my youngest sister to bid on the county's most sought after bachelor."

"Good thing you aren't in charge of me then, because I already planned to go to the auction. But now, I won't have to waste my precious future-predicting brain cells while trying to decide who has the privilege of getting my paddle in the air. That way, I won't have to bid on God's gift to man, Caleb Harlow."

"Avery..." I can already hear the lecture that's about to come out of his mouth.

"Chase, just stop," I cut him off. "I'll already be there, Courtney is bidding on Tommy, and it's a fundraising *group* date that's going to provide something our town desperately needs. It's been too long since Dr. Homes retired. Plus, I'm guessing Jackson has an ex or two he's trying to avoid. Problem solved."

He's quiet. That's a good sign. I think.

"You know the rule," he says.

"It's not a real date, you dink."

"Just a fundraiser?" He sounds less skeptical.

"Just a fundraiser with friends," I assure, keeping my voice placating.

"Fine."

I roll my eyes at his so-called acceptance.

"Don't worry about a second driver on Wednesday, I'll figure it out, okay?" I say to switch subjects before Chase can change his mind.

He lets out an audible huff, clearly unsure if he should let this situation rest or go on one of his rants about keeping his youngest sister away from ever possibly falling for Jackson Landen.

"Alright," he says.

"See you in a few days."

I hear him say "Mmm-hmmm," before we hang up.

I grab my bag and pop my phone in my pocket on my way out the door.

Chase doesn't know it, but he just gave me the best graduation gift I could have asked for: a date with Jackson Landen.

Chapter 2
Jackson

"When I suggested having you set up the stage instead, she said, and I quote, 'How selfish and petty would it look if I took him off the roster? Really, I'm doing Jacksy a favor,'" Chase says with the world's most placating expression on his face while doing a spot-on impression. Not that Sam would ever be caught dead wearing flannel and cowboy boots.

Or be seen in a horse stable.

Chet waves his goodbye, not bothering to hold in his laughter as he leaves for the day. I wonder how much I'd have to add to his wages to get him up on that stage instead of me.

"For fuck's sake," I mutter, thinking I was long past Sam's shit… and that nickname.

"You'll be fine. It's one group dinner. Your brother is going to be there, well, one of them, and Sam's got your cousin to handle the barbecue. It's practically a Landen family reunion."

"You're leaving out the fact that the barbecue is after an auction that you aren't being forced to partake in," I shoot back as my best friend talks me down from throwing the grooming brush across the stable.

"I can't help that Ava needed to snatch me off the market the moment she laid eyes on me," he says smugly.

I know he's trying to lighten the mood, but it just sours mine more. Knowing he has the woman of his dreams and I have… well, just dreams.

Misty flicks her tail so it brushes my arm and I know she can feel my agitation, automatically causing me to move towards her face.

"It's okay, girl," I mutter as I take a deep breath and press my face into the chestnut and white patches on her neck.

"Who's your sugar daddy?" Chase coos at Misty as he gives her yet another sugar cube. That horse has always had a soft spot for him.

I watch him for a moment. His hat is tipped up so his now-shaggy sun-bleached hair is pushed down on his forehead. He needs a shave and he looks tired. I feel a little guilty for being frustrated with him since his wife is having a rough first trimester. None of my brothers have kids yet, and I feel like an ass since he's taking care of her, slowly taking over the Barnett farm, and he still comes by to see me.

I sigh and put the brush away, patting Misty's flank while Chase rubs her white nose. He's such a suck-up. "I really have to do the auction?"

"I mean, you should. Sam would have never picked raising funds for new vet equipment if you hadn't made the case," he snorts. "Hey, since you've broken half the hearts in town, maybe Mrs. Fields can bid on you, and you'll have dinner with the world's snarkiest eighty-five-year-old at your side."

I glare at him.

"So, I just stand there, sweating bullets, while everyone watches me turn beet red praying that Mrs. Fields has stayed up late enough for the event so I don't have to spend the evening with an ex?" My hand is already forming a fist, so I shake it out.

"Nope," Chase says with a tone that tells me he could have said something to calm my anxiety when he walked in here five minutes ago. The dick.

"Go on..."

"Avery."

My heart stutters.

"What about her?" I choke out as I finish tidying up in Misty's stall. I can only imagine what my face would give away if I had been facing him.

"She's going to win the bid on you, so you don't have to worry about it."

I think my heart stops, but I force myself to keep moving.

"You're seriously going to make your baby sister bid on your best friend while she's finishing up her master's degree?" I ask incredulously, throwing in my usual "baby sister" to remind myself that she is, in fact, my best friend's youngest sibling. Because a six-year age gap was a lot while we were growing up, but now that she's twenty-five, there has been nothing "baby" about her for far too long.

"She'll be back at the end of the week, just in time to wave her MBA in my face before saving you from total embarrassment."

"And she agreed to this?" Shit, my palms are sweaty. I need to get it together.

He shrugs. "She called right after I saw Sam, and I filled her in, because if anyone besides yours-truly knows how to smooth your ruffled feathers, it's her." Fair enough. "And we both knew that you'd want to pull out. I didn't say a thing to her, she offered. I think she doesn't want to have questions about why she's not trying to snatch up a date with Caleb."

"What does Gary have to say about it?" I can't keep all the bitterness out of my tone as I tidy up Misty's stall an unnecessary amount. The one time she brought Gary home he was nothing but a pretentious ass.

"She ended things with him a while back. Said it was never going to really be anything." He says it casually, but I can feel his critical gaze on the back of my head.

He can't know. I've been so careful to keep this from him for the last five years. She was like a sister to me and then... she wasn't.

I wipe what must be ten different emotions off my face and turn while saying, "He was a dick. Good for her."

"We definitely agree on that," he says. "I don't have to say anything else about the whole 'winning a *date*' not really being a date, right?"

"She's *Avery*; she's like a sister to me," I lie through my teeth.

"Perfect," he says before cooing a goodbye to Misty. I keep tidying the now immaculate stall as he walks out of the stables.

I've never said a thing to anyone about Avery. I've never flirted with her or paid her any special attention. He likely thinks I'd fuck her and move right along to the next girl. I'm going to have to get my head on right before she moves back, or I'm going to be screwed.

I close Misty's door and lean against it, rubbing under her jaw as she nudges me with her nose.

"Well, girl, looks like your favorite human in the world might see you real soon," I murmur.

That makes two of us.

This is going to be the longest week of my life.

Chapter 3
Avery

Tommy Landen is sitting in a rocking chair on the front porch as I pull up to my family's main house. Instead of parking in the garage like usual, I stop near the steps before cutting the engine.

"What are you doing here?" I call as I get out of the car.

He makes a face like he ate something sour as he stands. "When did you start driving a sedan?"

"Well hello to you, too."

"You know what I mean. I'm obviously here to see you, but now I'm nervous that you turned into a true city girl."

"No, I borrowed Stacy's car since we're waiting on a part for my truck. I'm still a country girl through and through," I reassure him as he envelops me in a hug.

Well, it's more like he towers over me and tucks my head against his heart. I can smell something garlicky on him with the faint, but ever-present, smell of their ranch.

"You have a nice roommate, even if she's a city girl."

I know he didn't show up here to talk about my roommate.

"What's up, Tommy?" I prod him as we settle ourselves on the porch swing so we're side-by-side, his boots resting on the worn wooden floor while my toes barely touch.

"So, you know how you're bidding on Jax tonight?" he asks.

"Yeah. I told Chase I would to make sure he shows up, and so no one pressures me to bid on Caleb Harlow." It's so easy for these lies to sound natural.

He gives me a resigned look.

"Wait, how did you know that?"

"Courtney and I had lunch a few hours ago, and she mentioned it." He shrugs, trying to be nonchalant about something.

"Is there a crime that I'm missing about helping out your big brother so he won't end up spending the evening with an ex or Mrs. Fields? Or is this punishment for not being able to get back to Greenstone early enough to meet my two best friends?"

He sighs. "She said you're going to bid on Jax and I told her it might not be a great idea."

"What do you mean?"

"Trust me that this will make sense," he says wearily. He removes his white Stetson and I can see the apprehension in his bright blue eyes while he runs a hand through his almost-blond hair.

"Okay?"

"I've watched Jax over the years and, while he tries to hide it, he never fails to do one thing." He's looking at his hat now, which means he's definitely worried about how I might take this.

"And what is that?" I ask as I nudge him with my elbow so he looks at me.

"Notice you."

My heart pounds in my chest.

"It doesn't matter who's around or what's happening, he's pretty covert about it, but it's true. And I didn't want him to get the wrong impression about a pity bid when he has clearly, well, secretly, been hoping for a chance with you but could never risk taking it because of Chase."

"And you think—"

"I know. Courtney told me. She said it was a schoolgirl crush that never went away for you."

I don't even know what to say.

"I completely understand why you never said anything to me. I'm the second-youngest Landen and the guy you've been wanting has had a string of exes who never stay long."

"Tommy—"

"But he actually has a heart. You know how much I love you. And if it weren't just—"

"Tommy," I say more forcefully than necessary, which is enough to get him to pause. I sigh. "It hasn't been a schoolgirl crush since I was actually in high school."

"So, what are you saying? You've been over him for years? Then I really can't let you—"

"No, Tommy. Not over him." It's weird to admit it out loud to someone. Even Courtney doesn't know the full truth. It always felt too pathetic.

"What about Gary and Carter and —"

"I liked them all. Heck, I even loved some of them, but not the right kind of love. Not when..." I let myself trail off.

Tommy's quiet for a moment.

"Why the fuck haven't you said anything?" he practically shouts, slapping his hat against his leg with an incredulous look on his face.

"Because he's your *brother*. Because he can have, and pretty much has had, any person he wants. Because I'm his best friend's youngest sister—a friend who has been vehemently against him dating either Barnett girl."

"Minor details, Avery, minor," he says, waving away my concerns.

I can practically hear the gears turning in his mind and I can't help but smile at him.

"So, what's your game plan?"

"I'm bidding on him and I'm going to feel him out while giving fairly obvious signals," I venture.

"If Jackson thinks he's going to have a snowball's chance in hell with you, you're going to have to practically hit him over the head with a two-by-four."

"Jackson knows when a woman is interested in him."

"Not the one he's had his eye on and can never have. If you're giving him the green light, he's going to have to know that you mean it."

"I'll wear my "green means go" dress then, just to make everything all the more clear." He rolls his eyes at me before I add, "But that doesn't mean he's interested. He could have someone set to stop by his place after tonight's events."

"I doubt that very much. His schedule has, how do I put this delicately, thinned out significantly over the last year."

"Well, if he's interested, he's interested. If not, then I'll know." I'm not sure how that came out so casually when my heart is now thundering in my chest.

He puts his hat on and grabs my hand. "He is. You know I wouldn't have said anything if he wasn't."

The sincerity in Tommy's eyes gives me hope and I pull him in for a tight hug.

"Okay, let me know if you want me to do anything, but I need to get home and shower before the main event. See you tonight?"

"You know I wouldn't miss seeing you up on a stage for the world, Tommy," I call to him as he walks to the far side of the garage where he always parks, like it might ruin the view of the gardens or something.

This could either be the start of what I've dreamed of having for far too long, or a train wreck that only ends in heartbreak.

Chapter 4
Jackson

This shirt is stiff, and damn it, the tag is digging into the back of my neck again. This is why I hate new shirts.

And it's noisy. Why does everything have to be so goddamn noisy? For crying out loud, you'd think this was an animal auction, but instead of hearing hooves or clucking, it's chatter. So. Much. Chatter. And there's no hay.

My hand rests on my belt buckle, tracing the Landen Acres logo with the tips of my fingers, and things are a little less overwhelming in my head. I'm still second-guessing wearing it. I know Avery is just bidding on me to be nice, but something feels different. It just felt wrong to not wear the one gift I have from her, other than a rodeo ticket stub from when we sat next to each other, but I would look ridiculous having that with me.

I pull myself back to reality and look around from my place against the wall.

Sam is off to the side all gussied up as usual but has her clipboard in hand, studying it like she hasn't memorized every last damn detail. I shake my head. This is her world: being the biggest and brightest without officially making it all about her.

Tommy sidles up next to me and nudges me with his elbow. "How'd you ever let her out of your grasp, Jax?"

I try my best not to snort. "I think one month of being dressed up like a show pony was long enough."

"I still think you're a crazy fool for ending things." Tommy gives her a once over. "I figured if anyone in this town stood a chance at getting her to stay long term, it'd be you."

"I'm not exactly known for being the guy someone sticks around for."

"That might be true, but it definitely didn't end because one of you was already in love with someone else." He gives me a suspicious look and, for a second, I think he's talking about me. But no, definitely not.

"Are you suggesting that she was with the wrong Landen brother?" I don't know how I keep a straight face, but when I look at my younger brother, he's just watching Sam.

"Maybe," he mutters.

Stifling the joke I wanted to make about Bryant being the Landen brother for her, I smack him in the chest with the back of my hand, taking a different route. "You thinking about asking her out?"

That seems to shake him out of whatever dream world he went to.

"What? No. Absolutely not. Dating your ex would be weird."

It sounds like it's good that I didn't crack a joke about Bryant being the one for her.

"Would it?" I can't help but push his buttons a little and see him get all flustered. He always gets shy whenever Sam is around. He might actually have feelings for her.

Lord knows I'll take any distraction I can get from the stress of being around all these people and knowing that Avery is on the other side of those curtains. "Don't let me stand in your way."

"Ew. I would never—"

"Stop," I cut him off. "I never slept with her, so don't make things weird. Every time I told you I was her arm candy, I meant it. We had a public-event partnership that helped her meet people in town with minimal effort from me. Plus, it kept a few people who wanted 'seconds' off my back."

Tommy just looks at me like he's trying to balance chemical equations. "Huh."

"I said don't make it weird."

"Did you break things off because she wouldn't—"

"Seriously? You're asking me this here of all places?" I gesture around but try to keep my frantic motions close to my body so I don't draw attention our way.

"You're the one who just revealed that you were with someone you didn't sleep with," Tommy says with an incredulous look. "I'm just following your lead. Apparently, I only get all the good details when you're flustered from being in a crowd."

"You had to remind me, didn't you?" I crack my neck in an attempt to ease the building tension. "I'm going to step outside so I don't twitch on the auction block. Tell Sam?"

"I'm afraid you're going to have that honor. Courtney is determined to tame my cowlick and her chair just freed up." He slaps my arm as he hops over to his best friend's station. Well, one of his best friends. The other is apparently waiting to bid on me.

I can't focus on that right now. I imagine this is what the backstage area looks like for a beauty pageant. There are tables with makeup and hair products galore and mirrors with a dozen lights to practically blind the person in the chair. Thankfully, Courtney was extra fast with me, so I give her a smile before I head over to where Sam is standing.

"Thank you for wearing the shirt I sent over. I know how much you hate to wear things that aren't worn in, but as our second-to-last bachelor up for grabs tonight, I couldn't risk you showing up in something endearingly tattered."

She really doesn't need a conversation, just acknowledgement that you heard, so I nod and say, "I need to step out, but I'll be back before you kick things off."

She gives me a look I know all too well. "You're such a funny creature, Jacksy."

"I know," I say, itching to get out and away from everyone.

"You won't be late?"

"And ruin your entire event? Absolutely not."

With that, she tips her head towards the back door so I don't have to go through the crowd. It hits me that we never seemed capable of hating each other. It's not like there's any attraction anymore, if there ever was. Sure, she's a pretty girl, but that only carries you so far. I push the door open just enough to squeeze out and take a deep breath, leaning against the brick wall outside the auditorium.

I close my eyes after setting a five-minute timer and do my breathing exercises to calm my body. Not many things make me anxious, but I've always had a hard time staying calm and focused in crowds.

I relax my hands, letting them hang loose at my sides, and remind myself that I've known the people on the other side of this wall my whole life. Well, except for Sam and Caleb.

My fingers trace my buckle again, knowing the grooves by heart even though I don't wear it very often. I've held it enough to be able to create a perfect replica at this point. I open my eyes and look out to the horizon without turning my head, letting my eyes trace its lines from my left all the way to my right while silently counting to pace my breaths.

My alarm buzzes in my pocket and I realize how relaxed my shoulders are.

I turn off the alarm and notice a text.

Chase: You're up next, big guy. Don't forget to breathe and smile. Avery's here and she knows to bid quick so you can get it over with fast. I'm at the tables in the back sorting the cheesiest shit you've ever seen for a silent auction.

I like his message as I feel sweat trickle down the back of my neck. Damn it.

I reread it a few times just to see Avery's name tossed in there like it's natural to get updates on her.

I give myself one moment to picture Avery in the crowd, where she's waiting eagerly to bid on me. Just one moment where I imagine this was a proper date and Chase knew the truth. Just one moment where my best friend in the entire world knew I was actually capable of loving a partner.

And then I let reality sink back in.

Avery might be here, and she might be bidding on me, but I know it's just a plan she and Chase came up with to make sure I held up my end of the bargain to help raise funds for the new equipment.

She's not really here for *me*. She doesn't want more.

It doesn't matter that we're both single. It doesn't matter that she's finally moving back to Greenstone.

Hell, it doesn't matter that, however hard I try, I've never been able to love anyone else. How can you ever love someone else when your heart can't get over the girl you've never been able to have?

All that matters is that Avery is happy, and I don't lose my best friend.

With that sobering thought, I open the door and sneak back inside.

Chapter 5
Avery

Oh. My. God.

Tommy is putting on quite the show. I can almost ignore Sam's grating voice as she's talking about his education and proclivity towards math. I want to shout that he's an accountant—you can't make that sexy! But heckling is frowned upon and I don't need to draw attention to myself, at least not yet.

I make sure I raise my paddle a few times as the bidding starts, just to increase the already enthusiastic bidders. Everyone loves a Landen brother. I do love Tommy and want him to bring in a good amount after the year he's had. He's done a lot of healing, but I know his heart is still tender from Maisy leaving him for a bull rider. I don't blame him. After being with someone for three years, to then find out they were seeing someone else for at least eight months, would mess with anyone's heart.

I actually start laughing when he strikes another pose. It looks like he genuinely believes he's modeling right now, but he just looks ridiculous. That's Tommy for you. I smile up at him, even though there's no way he can see me. As the bidding climbs, the gavel strikes the wood and Sam shouts, "Sold!" into her microphone. Sam doesn't need a microphone. For someone so petite, she sure has a voice that carries when she wants it to.

I see Courtney do a little celebratory dance near the front. I put my thumb and middle finger into my mouth and give

Tommy a wolf-whistle as he blows Courtney a kiss and waves to the crowd before heading backstage. If I had a dollar for every time someone asks me if they're together, I'd be able to set my plans in motion for giving all the ranches sustainable growth models all by myself. Maybe I should charge people for an answer so Greenstone would be set for years to come.

Bringing myself back to reality, I attempt to look casual on my own. If anything, people are expecting me to bid on Caleb Harlow since he's the "fresh meat" in town. I've had a dozen people ask if we've been introduced already. There's a chance we have at some point, but I don't remember. I've seen him on the rodeo circuit and he and Matt Landen have hung out over the years. It seems like that friendship continued and, according to Tommy, Matt helped him choose his apartment in Greenstone.

I wish Courtney could stay out here for the auction, but she's already heading backstage for cleanup. Sam has to be just about ready to bring out Jackson.

Oh great. I'm pretty sure I'm blushing, which is horribly embarrassing. No one can actually see my heart beating through my chest, right? Because there are only two more bachelors for the auction, and I know Sam put the two participating Landen brothers back-to-back.

Which means I'm finally going to stake my claim on Jackson Landen. Just thinking about it keeps me thoroughly flushed. It's a good thing the spotlights mean the crowd is in a darker space.

I'm definitely second-guessing my plan. Maybe I could have thought of a less public way to show him that I want him? All of him.

Oh my God, can he say no? Are there rules that state someone can refuse a date?

I grab the little brochure on the counter next to me that explains the evening's activities, when my eyes are drawn back to the stage just in time to see the curtain pulled to one side. Jackson walks through, ducking his head like there might be a door frame that's low or something, which only makes me smile.

Damn, he looks amazing. The pearl-button-embroidered shirt is a little uppity for him, but at least it's flannel. The way it tapers from his chest to his waist accentuates how in shape he is. I let my eyes travel down his jeans, to his boots, and back up to his buckle. He's wearing his favorite "fancy belt" as he called it last Christmas, the one with his name inside the Landen Acres logo that I gave him for his thirtieth birthday.

Six years between us meant I was almost guaranteed to never have a chance with Jackson Landen, but I've dated enough boys to know he's the only man I want.

I stop gawking long enough to see his knuckles are already turning white and he has that look in his eyes that means he's not fully here. I don't know if he hears every tiny sound or if it's all a jumble, but he does this around crowds. Well, just crowds of people, not crowds of animals. He's at home with animals.

But he's smiling that gorgeous smile of his and attempting to look out at the crowd with his deep blue eyes. It's obvious none of the bachelors have been able to see anything—I swear Sam must have called every company in the tri-state area to find the brightest spotlights, ensuring each bachelor could be properly displayed.

Well, I'll give her credit for properly displaying Jackson Landen because he looks incredible. Granted, I think he looks fantastic covered in dirt and dust with hay stuck to his clothes after mucking out the stables, but tonight, his hat is tipped back just enough so we can see his face, right down to the little scar that runs through one eyebrow. His hair is usually short, but I'm guessing Courtney gave him a trim, because the sides are tapered more than usual from his beard to the brown tuft that I know would be curly if he ever let it grow out. Not one of the other four Landen brothers has curly hair, but their mom does, so he must have gotten it from her.

I let the first round of bidding go without moving my arm. I know there are plenty of men and women here who want a chance with Jackson, and for more than I'd like to think about, a second chance. But that's okay, I can let them tire themselves out.

When Sam is only calling out two numbers, I finally raise my paddle. In that moment I can feel just about everyone's eyes shift to me. I focus on keeping my expression calm. I'm just bidding on my brother's best friend. There's nothing weird or out-of-character about this.

Yeah, right.

The other bidder drops out, so it's just me and Mrs. Fields, who has been quite persistent with her paddle each time someone bids on Jackson. I might have to bake her some lemon sparkle cookies this weekend to soothe her ego, because I'm not letting her win tonight.

I take a sip of my water so I don't look as desperate as I feel for this bidding war to be over. I'm not bowing out, but if Mrs.

Fields doesn't back down soon, it's going to look like I'm a woman on a mission.

Which I am, but no one needs to know that.

I can feel Chase's eyes on me from where he's organizing the last-minute silent auction items. If there's one positive thing about Ava being so nauseous during her first trimester, it's that everything she volunteered for now falls to Chase, keeping him off my back for likely looking like some crazed woman at this point.

The dollars keep adding up. Holy shit, she's going strong. I might as well buy the equipment on my own.

I'm getting close to reminding Mrs. Fields that she's been married six times already and Jackson isn't going to be number seven, when she finally keeps her paddle down, giving me a look that tells me she knew I wasn't going to let her have it.

Well played. I nod towards her, and she winks back before composing her features into a slightly disgruntled expression, while everyone is clapping for how much was just raised. At least I got paid this week.

We're well over halfway funded now, so if my plan goes to complete shit, at least I can say I did something right tonight.

Jackson does a little wave, still looking lost as ever, before turning to slip behind the curtain, giving everyone a fantastic view of his ass. The man couldn't look sexier in jeans.

Time to go make sure my date doesn't sneak out early to be with his horses.

Chapter 6
Jackson

I try to see if I can find Avery, or more likely Chase, since she's only five feet tall, but the only person I can see besides Sam is Mrs. Fields, who looks slightly put out. I give her a smile as I wave to whoever is out there, like I have a clue about what just happened, and turn to get behind the curtain again.

"Are you kidding me, man?" Tommy is in my face immediately.

"Tell me it wasn't terrible."

"Weren't you able to listen?" he asks.

"It all got fuzzy again, but I know whoever has paddle 43 got the bid."

"So you didn't hear the bidding? Man, it was epic!" He's all animated now that he's in full story-teller mode. "I can't believe you missed it! Mrs. Fields was bidding against Tanya Jenkins and Avery."

My heart starts a new rhythm just hearing her name. This is not good. I need to get things under control before I see her, or Chase is going to be all over me. Tommy and I walk off to the side where things are a little calmer.

"Tanya dropped out after about six rounds, and I've never seen Mrs. Fields as cranky as she was when Avery kept outbidding her. Eventually she conceded, and you just brought in almost a third of the funding goal! Well, I should say that Avery just donated almost a third of the funding goal."

"Well, Chase said she would bid on me so I wasn't stranded and we both know how she gets when she sets her mind to something."

"Sure, Jax, that's *definitely* why she didn't drop out when there was already healthy bidding happening." Tommy rolls his eyes.

"Dude, she's Chase's baby sister who did her brother's-best-friend a solid favor so I wouldn't have to spend the evening with anyone I'm trying to avoid." I couldn't leave out the "baby," especially when I knew I'd be seeing her in a matter of minutes.

"Yeah, you keep telling yourself that. But go outside before the mingling happens." He looks down pointedly at my knuckles.

I hadn't realized my right hand was in a tight fist from the onslaught of sounds while my eyes finished adjusting to dim backstage lighting conditions.

I just nod and slip out again, setting a timer for five minutes before letting my head fall back against the bricks once more, only hearing muted sounds from the other side of the door.

The only problem is that now, I have the space to fixate on what Avery was thinking. I know she can be competitive, but if Tommy was right, she was in it to win it.

Well, to win *me*.

I wonder if Chase goaded her into higher and higher bids. There's no way he'd have let me go for cheap, mostly so he'd have bragging rights about what his best friend brought in for the donations.

I hear the door open and turn to see my favorite green eyes on a freckled face, and my heart skips a beat.

"I knew I'd find you out here." Avery smiles at me.

"You know me well," I reply, unable to say anything else. She looks amazing. She's got on one of her little sundresses with skinny straps that you could probably snap with your teeth. This one is green and it loosely falls over her incredible curves. It's tighter on top to show off her ample cleavage.

I realize I'm staring at her like an absolute creep, so I shake my head and shift my gaze towards the horizon and try to hide what's happening in my pants. Jesus, this girl turns me into an eighteen-year-old who's visiting his first strip club.

"How did Caleb do?" I ask.

"Didn't stay to watch. I thought I'd make sure my date didn't sneak back to his horses." She leans against the wall, close enough that I can feel her body heat through my sleeve. I'm already so wound up I'm not sure what I should be doing. I just know that right now, with her next to me, I feel calm. And horny as hell.

"Nah, I would never abandon you." I quickly add, "Or Mrs. Fields."

She smirks at me. "I'm sure she'd be happy to know that."

We stand there for a minute, watching the colors change in the sky. She shifts just a little and her arm presses against mine and I hold my breath for a moment so I don't react. She has never given me clear signals. Unlike Chase, who has left room for no questions about how he feels about me ever dating his little sister. He knows almost everything about me, including how I've never been able to tell a girl I loved her. He just doesn't know why. Honestly, I didn't realize it until the night of the rodeo.

I give myself a moment to look over at the one reason I couldn't give my heart to anyone else. She had it long before I ever realized.

I take a slow breath to clear my mind. The silence is easy with Avery, but I want to hear her voice and her laugh.

"Thanks for bidding on your brother's best friend." I wince at my words.

She makes a soft noise in her throat like she's amused and replies, "I figured it was about time we went on a date." She keeps her gaze on the sky as I watch her, my stomach knotting.

"What do you mean?" I can't help but ask, needing confirmation.

"You're awfully cute when you pretend to be ignorant." She pats my arm, and I don't respond.

She can't know. Even if she somehow had feelings for me, there's no way she knows about mine. I haven't told anyone. I've acted like a big brother around her. Haven't I?

"Courtney told me your cousin is handling the barbeque tonight."

How can she just change the subject like that when I'm floundering?

Get it together, Jax.

"Yeah, he's got his own giant smoker so he can finally take everything on the road." My brain is still trying to sift through what she said about me pretending to be ignorant.

"As long as he brings his famous honey barbecue chicken, I don't care how or where he makes it." She pats her stomach, bringing my gaze back to that dress. It's got little flowers stitched in the same shade of green.

I hear her suppress a giggle and drag my gaze up to find her staring right at me with a smile that tells me she's trying not to laugh at me obviously checking her out. I'm positive my cheeks are red as I roll my eyes and try to have a conversation like a normal human being. "Yeah, his chicken is great."

Way to go, Jax. That'll show her you weren't just thinking about how she'd look without that green dress on.

"Uh-huh," is her only reply, and I swear she lets out a little snort.

"Dork," I say as I nudge her with my elbow, trying to regain that "brotherly" vibe.

She rests her head against my arm. She's too short to reach my shoulder, but I don't dare move.

"Whatever you say, Jackson." And there it is. When Chase and I were finishing our college classes, she started calling me Jackson. Not Jay, not Jax, but Jackson. Not even my parents called me that. Just her. And it makes my heart gallop in my chest to hear her say it.

My phone vibrates and I have to reach into my pocket to shut off my alarm. She glances over to see the time and simply grabs my hand, tugs the door open, and says, "Come on, I got you."

And just like that, I'm like a puppy dog happily following behind, willing to do whatever Avery wants and probably more.

Chase is going to kill me.

Chapter 7
Avery

I give myself a moment to really look at Jackson before we head back inside. My hand feels tiny in his and I barely come up to his chest, so to look at his face means I have to tip my head back. He seems nervous, which is pretty out of character for him, but I'm guessing Chase made sure to mention the whole Avery-is-off-limits thing when he told him I'd be winning the bid. I can see his jaw working before meeting his eyes, which are searching my face.

Well, I'm not going to announce all of my feelings for him here and now, so I just nod, give him a smile, and head through the door. The poor guy lets me gently pull him back to the auditorium. I can feel his hand getting a little sweaty, so I steer us to where I hear Tommy's laughter over the rest of the sounds.

Jackson pauses and I can feel the tension rolling off of him as he drops my hand like I just branded him. I turn and see he's staring off in the direction of the auction tables that Chase is in charge of. The crowd would have to part for me to have a chance at finding him over there, so I know there's no way Chase could see us holding hands. But if he somehow managed it, I can only imagine the look Chase is giving him.

Resisting the urge to roll my eyes, I grab his elbow, getting his attention. "Come on, your brother is off to the side."

He hesitates for a moment before giving me a tight nod and I lead us through the crowd over to Tommy and Courtney, who are laughing about something, as usual.

"Hey! He didn't sneak off to spend the evening with Misty!" Tommy ribs.

Jackson just lets out a huff of annoyance but doesn't pull his arm out of my grasp.

"Jackson, you should have seen Tommy up there!" Courtney begins. "Don't get me wrong, I'm sure you were an absolute delight to watch with those spotlights on you, but I swear your little brother was about to take off his shirt to keep the bidding going."

This gets him to crack a smile and I snort out a laugh because that is totally something Tommy Landen would do if given the chance.

"I bet you would've gotten Mrs. Fields to put up a fight if you had done that."

"Now she'll have to go to bed thinking about what she missed out on." Tommy sighs dramatically.

"Will she ever survive?" Courtney deadpans and Tommy mock-glares at her.

I rub my thumb against Jackson's biceps. Good Lord, I don't think this man has one inch on his body that isn't perfect.

"Who's ready for the main event? I'm starving!" Tommy says as he rubs his hands together enthusiastically.

"Says the guy who just ate my granola bar."

"You pack those just for me and you know it."

Courtney shakes her head. "Someone has to make sure you don't get hangry. How the hell are you ever going to get a girlfriend if you're a drama queen half the day?"

"You do keep the best granola bars with you."

I feel Jackson stiffen right before I hear, "Courtney restocked and didn't tell me?" Chase's face pops into our little circle on the other side of Jackson's broad shoulders.

"What is with grown-ass men not being able to plan ahead?" gripes Courtney as she reaches into the bag in question and pulls out another granola bar, which she dramatically hands over to Chase's eager hand.

"You're a doll."

My brother tears the wrapper open with teeth and freezes. He's staring at my hand tucked in Jackson's arm and I feel Jackson start to panic.

Oh, hell no. I'm not backing off just to play nice around my stubborn-ass brother. Especially not when I just beat out most of the women, and a few of the men, here.

Chase pointedly clears his throat and stares me down.

Jackson starts to take a step to the side and I give his arm a tug and hold firm.

"You knew perfectly well that I was winning a date with Jackson, and you were completely on board with it. Calm down."

Jackson's now as stiff as a board.

I can see Chase's jaw working before flashing me a sour grin. "I didn't say a thing, little sis."

"Ew. First, we're not going back twenty years for nicknames. Second, you don't always have to speak to say something. Third, you're not the boss of anyone here. Know that you've been heard loud and clear. By everyone. So put a lid on it."

Shit, I hope I didn't just push him too far and open the doors for a Barnett sibling throw down. We haven't yelled at each other in years and it would be ridiculous for us to lose our cool here.

"How's Ava feeling tonight?" Tommy asks.

Oh, I could kiss Tommy Landen right on the mouth because nothing softens my brother up faster than talking about his wife. His now-pregnant wife.

"Still nauseous most of the day, but we've almost hit the second trimester. Daffodil has become a sentry on duty and even switched to the floor on Ava's side of the bed instead of mine." He shakes his head and smiles at the thought of that dog, who truly hated all men except him. Daffodil has been head-over-heels for Chase since Ava moved in with her uncle next door.

Even if Daffodil had hated Chase from the start, he would have found a way to win her over because the moment Ava stepped out of her car to move into her uncle's house, he was an absolute goner.

The conversation goes on without me as my mind drifts to what Jackson is feeling after what I said to Chase. A quick glance tells me he's still a little tense but his hand isn't in a fist, which means he's not panicking. My eyes take in all of him and then land on the buckle. I took my Landen Acres shirt to a local artist I heard about near campus with the adjustments I was hoping to have done. She was able to create a one-of-a-kind buckle for him. It has the family's horseshoe logo, but instead of it saying

Landen Acres, I had her fill in the sides of the horseshoe and put his name in the middle. I didn't want everyone to know what went into the gift and it was easy enough to pretend I found some random store online who could spit them out by the dozen. Judging by the way he held it at his birthday party, he knew it wasn't an afterthought.

I look up at him and see the man I fell for years ago and know that my fingers wrapped around his biceps might not mean the same to him as it does to me. I know if Jackson really does want me, even a fraction of the way I want him, my brother is going to be a brick wall for us to go through. Especially after the mini-scene he just caused over me having my hand on his arm. But there's something different. I might be an absolute fool, but even if we have to hide until Chase can be reasoned with, I feel like I might actually have a chance with Jackson Landen.

He peeks down at me and gives me a hint of a smile before Sam is back on her microphone announcing that the transportation to the group date for the auction winners is just out the side door.

"We still on for tomorrow?" Jackson asks Chase.

"I'll be over before kickoff."

I see Chase shift into protective-brother-mode, but before he can say anything to me, I catch his eye and say, "Group date. Get over it."

Jackson looks like he's trying to not laugh at the incredulous face Chase gives me in response.

"Group gathering," Chase replies as he heads back over to help keep the bidding active for the silent auction. I'm sure he can hear me rolling my eyes as we head our separate ways.

Tommy and Courtney lead the way to where we find a big yellow school bus waiting for us.

Both Jackson and Tommy just groan.

Chapter 8
Jackson

"Y**ou** sure are in a hurry," I venture.

"To get away from Chase and make sure we don't miss our luxury transport? Absolutely," she says with a grin.

"And why would we need to get away from Chase?" I ask playfully, even though my heart seems to be beating a million miles an hour.

She stops to face me in front of the big yellow school bus—our fancy wheels to the barbeque. "Again, you're cute when you pretend to be oblivious."

She turns around and shifts so she's holding my hand once more and I gladly oblige because I want nothing more than to be right about my suspicions that she feels the same way I do. Especially after how she responded to Chase only moments ago.

Right now I have a whole lot of hope that I'm reading even just a few of her signals right. If I'm wrong, well, I can let myself pretend on this fundraiser date.

Even before I ascend the first step, I know that men over six feet tall should not be allowed to step onto school buses. Tommy looks comical with his hat hitting the ceiling. I at least take mine off so I can avoid ducking most of the way. We stop at the seat behind Tommy and Courtney, who are already laughing about something, and Avery motions for me to get in first. I just look at the seat trying to figure out how all of my six feet plus a few inches are going to fold up into this tiny space.

"Go on," Avery says, nudging me to the left with her hip.

I throw myself in at an angle with my legs somehow staying on this side of the aisle. I have no idea how I manage this, and my hat is barely above the top of the seat because I'm at such an awkward angle against the wall, but by the time I pull my feet in so I don't trip the next few couples, Avery has hopped right next to me with a smirk before leaning her back against my side. Oh God, she smells amazing. I swear there's a hint of peach and I want to bury my face in her hair. Well, I want to bury my face in a lot of places on Avery Barnett, but I'd rather not have my best friend castrate me. She's one package of pure curvy temptation wrapped up in a little green sundress and she's leaning against me in a seat with no wiggle room. What the hell am I supposed to do now?

"That wasn't so hard now, was it?" says the girl who tops out at five feet. She gives me a smirk before shifting so her head rests on my chest, like it's the most natural thing.

Lord, she is either going to give me a heart attack or way too much to think about tonight in the shower. But instead of panicking over Chase, who has been there for me my entire life, I breathe in that faint peach smell. Maybe I'll regret this in about two seconds, but I let myself relax, dropping my arm from the top of the seat so my hand rests on her hip.

Avery places her hand on my leg and it takes everything in me not to unravel in this very moment. I instantly tense, not knowing how to handle this situation.

But before I can even think about setting up boundaries with my best friend's baby sister, the one person who Chase has made abundantly clear I shall never date because of my horrible record with both men and women, I need to know what the hell she's thinking. Because if she's just messing with me, I can lock my heart down. But if she's not, which is highly unlikely, then I need to find a way to tell Chase the one secret I've kept from him for too many years.

I take a chance and put my hand on top of hers.

"Took you long enough," she whispers.

I can hear the smile in her voice as she touches her cheek to my chest. I tip my head down so only Avery will hear me.

"I can't decide if you've been messing with me, or if you're actively trying to get your brother to kill me," I murmur, intentionally close so she can feel my breath on her ear.

She shudders against me and I feel confident in two things. One, that Avery isn't playing me. And two, I'm definitely going to need a moment to adjust myself when we all stand up.

"I'll figure Chase out," she says as she stretches her neck, exposing what I want to run my tongue along.

"I don't think it works like that, baby," I say against her ear, clearly playing with fire as some of my usual confidence comes back in this little bubble of privacy we seem to have. The word that I've used for years to remind myself she can't be mine comes out in a new context— one that I don't know she's ready for, but I'm so jumbled up right now, I know I'm not thinking clearly. My voice is husky and I can't help it one bit.

She moves the hand on my thigh up higher and squeezes as she presses harder against me before whispering, "Only call me that if you plan to make me yours."

"Fuck me."

I don't realize the words left my mouth until she turns around to face me. She puts her hand on my cheek and I hold completely still. Waiting.

She makes sure my eyes are locked with hers as the bus slows before saying, "Here's hoping, Jackson Landen."

My mind is racing with every little thing I've dreamt of doing with Avery and it takes all of my willpower to not tangle my fingers in her auburn hair and claim every square inch of her.

Her thumb shifts on my cheek so she can run it along my lower lip. I don't even hesitate to grab it between my teeth and swirl my tongue around it for a second, imagining it's her clit as her eyes flutter closed and I release it.

I remember that we're on a bus full of people from this small town. However, we seem to be wildly lucky because no one seems to be paying any attention to what's happening in our seat. I guess it's a good thing I'm in such a ridiculously slouched position.

Something shifts in her eyes as she puts her hand on my chest and asks, "What are you doing Wednesday?"

What?

"Um, nothing scheduled." My voice is still deeper than usual even with this abrupt shift.

"Perfect." Her hand slides a little south, making me forget that I can't throw her down on this seat and sink deep inside her. "How would you feel about driving out to my apartment and helping with my final load?"

How the fuck does this sound sexy? Did I hear her right?

"You... want me to help you move back home?" I ask, trying to figure out if this is some game, but I can't concentrate with her hand on my abs. Fuck, I'm acting like a teenager who's never gotten laid.

"Mmm-hmm, Chase and I will finish boxing things up on Tuesday and then everything can be loaded and hauled Wednesday."

Well that was the bucket of ice water I needed to shut things down.

Chapter 9
Avery

Jackson grabs my wrist and sits straighter. Well, as much as a guy whose legs are at such a weird angle can.

"Avery." His tone is frustrated as he frowns.

And I immediately realize how this looks.

"Shit. No," I blurt. "Oh fuck, that all came out wrong."

He totally thinks I was trying to seduce him to get help moving home.

I fully shift so my legs are under me, knees touching his thigh so I'm not twisting to face him. He drops my wrist and I grab his hand because whatever was brewing between us wasn't some fantasy; it was real, and I can't let him think it wasn't.

"I was going to ask you tomorrow if you might be available to help. I had everything planned out." He looks at me with one eyebrow raised. "No, really. I even bought everything to bake oatmeal chocolate chunk cookies."

He looks slightly less skeptical. "Go on…"

I can't tell him what I was actually thinking while running my hands lower on his stomach, not here, so I settle for a partial truth. "They're still waiting for the part to come in for my truck and I need to return my roommate's car. Chase's truck can fit most of my things but not all of them. I know that this one," I nod toward Tommy who has been chatting animatedly with Courtney this entire time, "has his little Q&A at the high school with the senior math classes, but I know that you typically have minimal things to handle on Wednesdays."

"And all of this," he moves our hands to indicate the space between us, "was to butter me up?"

He's not scoffing at me, so that has to be a good sign, right?

"No. Not at all. I wouldn't butter you up for a favor." And my mind goes down a quick rabbit hole of what it would be like to lick butter, or whipped cream, off the abs my hand was so recently touching.

Focus.

He looks slightly amused at how flustered I am right now.

"So what was it?" he asks point-blank.

"This," I move our hands just like he did, "is exactly what it looked like before my brain caught up with my tongue."

His eyes shoot down to my lips before meeting my gaze again, this time with some of that heat back.

"This," I say putting my hand on his abs once more, "gave me an idea that one does not speak of while on a school bus meant to transport children. But that thought was tied to driving. Well, not me driving. But me in the front seat."

"With Chase driving?"

"Oh, God no!" I say, horrified. "No. Something that my brother can have nothing to do with, but I think might make the trip worth your while."

"Avery, I have no idea what's happening in that mind of yours, but you do know that you won't ever owe me anything, right?"

"Jackson, this little something is more for me than it would be for you." I try to not give him a look that makes me feel like an absolute hussy because I'm actually salivating thinking about what I can do to him while he's driving if my brother can't see us.

"But there will be oatmeal chocolate chunk cookies?" he asks.

"Of course," I respond solemnly. "Unless your tastes have changed?"

He gives my hand a squeeze. "No, Avery, my tastes haven't changed one bit."

And I don't think he's talking about cookies.

Lord, I want to kiss this man and rip open that shirt, sending those pearl buttons all around the bus.

"Perfect, mine haven't either," I reply.

The bus hits a bump as we transition to the gravel road leading us to the park and we both take a breath in.

"Damn it, my mouth is watering already," I say, realizing it's probably been a full year since I've had Jesse's famous barbecue chicken.

"Mine, too," he replies with his eyes on my mouth.

Tommy opens the window to catcall his cousin as our bus turns around the bend. We see the park up ahead and Jesse's food truck is there with the smoker letting off a constant gray cloud. I shift so my ass is back on the seat and so I can lean against Jackson for the last minute of the ride. If I'm not careful, I'm going to need a dry pair of panties because being this close to Jackson has me unbelievably turned on.

How the hell am I going to not grope this man at a public picnic?

Chapter 10
Jackson

The bus comes to a stop, and I give Avery's hip a squeeze to keep her here while I let my mind fixate on what just happened.

"If there's a chance this is a game, please tell me now." I know it isn't the smoothest thing to say but any semblance of privacy is about to go out the window and I'm going to lose my mind second-guessing and reading into every little thing she does.

She stands up and holds out her hand as if she's going to lift me out of this seat.

"Jackson, if there are any games involved in this," she says, waiting for me, "I'm only playing for keeps."

Well, fuck. I got my answer, I guess.

I feel like a lumbering giant getting out of this tight space. But the walk down the narrow aisle does afford me the chance to stare at her ass without shame for a full five seconds before we're descending the stairs.

Jesse has the tables piled high with corn, slaw, potato salad, and so much meat already that I can't even imagine what's still in the smoker.

"Avery Jo you sure are a sight for sore eyes. How does it feel to have mastered business administration?" Jesse calls out.

She just laughs as he pulls her in for a hug and congratulates her. I love seeing how proud she is.

Nope. I can't afford to actually let myself live in a fantasy where I get to... Damn it. Snap out of it.

I slap Jesse on the shoulder and tell him he's outdone himself with the feast. I feel a now-familiar hand slip into mine as Avery says, "We don't want Tommy to steal all the chicken."

Jesse just grins at me and mouths *That's new,* and I give him a helpless look as I'm once more tugged towards a mountain of food waiting for all thirty of us.

"Dig in, everyone! Sam told me to make sure you eat while it's hot. She'll be closing out the silent auction, so she won't be out for the food or the games—"

"What a shame," murmurs Avery and I hold back a smile. She's jealous of someone I basically buddied up with for a month. I'll have to remember to explain what our arrangement was.

"But the coolers are full and we *shouldn't* run out of food. So just let me know if you need anything and enjoy," Jesse says.

We approach the eating area and I notice the picnic tables have benches that can't be pulled out. Once more Sam has neglected to think of something that people over six feet have issues with. But Avery moves me to the other side of her so I have an end seat as she neatly sits herself down on the bench beside me, tucking her dress under her incredible ass. It's taking more self-control than I care to admit to not act on the lust that's been building over the years.

Once more, I need to remind myself of what this would do to my best friend. Chase, just think of Chase and how many ways he'll bring me back from the dead just so he can kill me over and over. Whatever this may or may not be, I'm not stupid enough to risk a lifetime of friendship over something that can't even be discussed right now.

Courtney and Tommy are across from us, which relaxes me. And then I realize I'm not tense after being on a noisy bus and now at a barbecue with thirty people. I have either been too distracted by Avery, or she's somehow helping me cope with my issue with groups of people. She's making this whole affair something I don't have to sit and literally sweat through.

I glance at her as she's piling Jesse's barbecue chicken onto her plate before looking down at mine to hide my smile. She has loved his chicken since he started trying out different recipes. My first bite tonight is an explosion of flavor; it's truly the best chicken I've ever eaten. It's juicy with a good crisp on the skin and you start with a salty-sweet flavor that gets spicier as you chew, but it never leaves you reaching for your drink.

I can't even pretend to ignore Avery as she takes her first bite of chicken. "Oh my God," she moans. "I missed this so much."

Once again, I'm grateful we're sitting down, even if it's at these ridiculous tables, so no one can see how turned on I am by this woman.

Tommy effortlessly keeps the conversations going before diving into a topic that I'd happily never talk about again.

"So Avery, now that you're back, I'm gonna need the actual in-person details from what went down with Gary because you've pointedly neglected sharing them via text."

"There's nothing much else to say," she responds. "We both knew that whatever we were doing wasn't permanent."

"Huh. I guess we all figured when you left for your last semester that you'd return home with a diploma and a ring,"

Tommy says, and Courtney back-hands his chest before my brain can catch up with his meaning.

A fucking ring? No one ever said anything about Avery marrying that ass. Who cares if Chase might kill me? I'll be going to jail for murdering my own brother soon.

But instead of being pissed, Avery just says, "I appreciate you working so hard to make sure things are crystal clear, Tommy, but I think the message has been delivered."

What? My mind races back to the conversation Tommy and I had earlier this evening as I try to put the pieces together. Courtney just coughs, clearly covering up a laugh, while Tommy smirks at Avery before he winks at me, actually winks, as he tears into his ribs. I'm definitely going to have a word with my younger brother on the way home about what he already seems to know.

Courtney is now silently laughing and trying to make it look like she's deciding what to stab with her fork next. Avery puts her hand on my thigh, again, like it's normal, and quietly says, "Don't over-analyze."

"I seem to be out of the loop on something." I lean down so she can only hear me.

"They're just trying to help."

"Is this a coordinated attack?" I ask.

"No, just a solo mission with some cheerleaders."

"Anyone else aware of this so-called mission besides these two?"

"Nope." And she gives me that smile that I would do anything for.

Chapter 11
Avery

The next two hours go by too quickly.

It's one thing to be able to grab Jackson's hand to bring him through a crowd or hold his arm right after winning the group date with him, but it's another thing entirely to be all over him during the whole event. At least the bus gave us an excuse to be close. Even Courtney and Tommy were squished together in their shared seat. That's just what happens when you've got yourself a Landen brother with you.

But playing cornhole and ladder ball without having a reason to touch him just drags everything out. Like foreplay, but without the climax.

God, I have to get my mind refocused or I really am going to jump Jackson in public.

Thankfully, Tommy and Courtney are around and they keep insisting that Jackson and I are paired up against them. Before we know it, we're back on the bus heading into town.

"You ready?" Jackson asks, offering me his arm.

Apparently, all I needed to get the guy's attention was to actually show I'm interested. Well, knowing that I'm finally back in Greenstone for good and not bouncing between undergrad, my internships, and then grad school may have also played a huge part. At least now people shouldn't bat an eye at our age gap, right?

Shit. I guess there was a lot mentally holding me back from trying to be with Jackson. But now I can honestly say this isn't some fleeting crush that's going away.

Again, we're behind my two best friends, but this time we have seats in the very back since everyone else piled into the front, exhausted and full from the evening. So now I'm thinking of all the things I could try without being seen...but I have plans for some of that on Wednesday.

Jackson flops into the seat first and I resist the urge to crawl on my hands and knees until I'm able to straddle him.

Instead of attempting to have my way with him, I just tuck myself in like I did before, but this time, as I lean against him, he drops his arm right away. Just feeling his hand rubbing my hip right next to my tattoo makes me want to squirm because I have no idea how he'll react to it. I never thought he'd see it when I got it. It was my attempt to leave Landen Acres in the past before I finally agreed to go on a date with Gary.

He tips his hat down so it almost looks like he's napping as he slouches a little more in the seat.

"So, Wednesday is the day you're officially home?" he asks.

"Yeah." I know Barnett Farm is my home, but something about my answer feels a little funny.

"And you'd like me to drive all the way to the big city just so you can watch me haul furniture?"

"Pretty much," I say, hiding my smile.

"It's a good thing I've been throwing hay bales around for more than half my life."

"You've been preparing for this moment without realizing," I say, unable to conceal a giggle.

His arm tucks me into his side a little more and I can feel his chest move as he chuckles.

"What time would you like me to show up?" he asks.

"Would one or two work? Or is that not enough time to get your morning chores done?"

"Yeah, that'll be fine. Misty has a little more company right now because one of our stallions is recovering from an injury, so my routine doesn't take much longer than usual. I can leave before noon for sure."

"Which stallion? Is he okay?" I ask.

"It's a new one that Matt picked up a few weeks ago, he's been cranky since he needs to take it easy and he's a lot calmer in the small stables."

"That's because Misty's the best horse out there. Who wouldn't want to be near her?"

"I can't think of anyone," he replies.

We fall into silence, but it's easy and comfortable. I reach my hand across my stomach until our fingers entwine. And this feels different than me pulling him along as the guy I bid on. This just feels like *us*.

And as much as I want to explore every inch of this man, which I've wanted to do since I turned eighteen, this feels safe—like this can last.

It feels like *this* is something that can weather the storm that will be known as Hurricane Chase.

I know I told him to leave Chase to me, but my brother is as stubborn as I am. I know what Jackson has allowed him to see and what he's hidden from his best friend. And if anyone can hold a grudge, it's a Barnett.

He squeezes my hand when we're in town. I hadn't noticed because I had let my eyes fall shut, breathing in the spicy-sweet smell that is Jackson. I sit up and he adjusts his hat, giving me a wink as he keeps his arm around me.

"I assume texting or calling isn't the best idea just yet?" he asks.

"Probably not, but I'll send you the address. We'll think of something Chase can't stumble across."

Before the bus parks and we all head home, he nods and tucks me into him so his chin rests on top of my head. "We'll figure it out."

"And we'll be moving me back home in just a few days."

"Good," he says. "You'll be where you belong soon enough."

For some reason, I don't think he's talking about Barnett Farm, and that makes me feel all tingly.

Chapter 12
Jackson

E ven though my body is ready to cramp up from slouching in this seat for privacy, getting out of this seat is just about the last thing I want to do right now. I've got the girl of my dreams tucked against me once more and this time we're holding hands. It might not seem like much, but I feel like I've been in the desert for far too long and just found an oasis.

I'm not sure what happens after we get her back home. I just know that, as I squeeze her hand once more, this isn't some fluke. I can be patient.

She gets out of the seat and waits for me before she reaches back and our fingers fall right into place as she leads the way one more time tonight. When we get to the steps, she looks back at me with a soft smile. "See you Wednesday?"

I know this is where our little bubble needs to burst and I tighten my hold on her hand before saying, "See you Wednesday."

She nods and hops out of the bus, joining Courtney and Tommy who put their arms around her as they say goodnight. I wouldn't normally be in the middle of that, so I unlock my SUV as I walk over. I can hear her laughter carry through the chaos and I give myself a second to look back as I grab the door handle. God damn, she's beautiful.

I hear footsteps getting closer as I get into the driver's seat and shut my door. Tommy hops into the passenger seat as I turn on the ignition. I don't think I've really said much today, to be honest, but my head is swimming.

I glance at him before pulling out of the parking spot at the auditorium and Tommy is failing at hiding his smile.

"Not a word," I mumble at him.

"Me?" Tommy fake gasps. "Why would I say anything about my big brother who has clearly been in love with his best friend's sister, who happens to be *my* best friend, but somehow the little woman is as sneaky as they come and neglected to tell me—"

"I said NOT a word." But I'm pretty sure even my ears are red after hearing half of that spoken out loud.

I glare at him, which only makes him laugh.

"You are so fucked, Jackson."

"I..."

"Yes?" He's batting his eyes at me.

"Nothing."

"Au contraire, brother dearest. See, where Bryant would let you run scenario after scenario through your racing mind, *I'm* the brother who can actually help you get the one thing you've been pining for. Even if it's always when you think no one is looking."

"How are you...aware...of anything that has happened, or not happened, for that matter?" I ask carefully.

At this he softens, which might be worse than his taunting.

"I talked to Avery after finding out she was going to bid on you."

"Why?"

He sighs. "Because I knew how you felt. And, no, I don't think other people, including Chase, have picked up on it. But, over the years, I've seen the way you look at her, and only when you were confident no one was paying attention. As the dorky *second*-youngest, but clearly the most handsome, Landen brother, I have the ability to slip under the radar." He shrugs, but I know he's sensitive about being looked over. He thinks being so gifted in math, when the rest of us would much rather muck out the stalls for a year than handle the books, isn't a desirable quality compared to the sheer bulk of Bryant, the boyish charm of Matt, or the cocky confidence of Chuck.

"Okay..."

"So, I stopped by their farm so I could catch her when she got home, knowing Chase would be setting up tables already." He pauses. "I may have asked her to *not* bid on you."

I just let the silence stretch, not knowing what to do with that information.

"I knew there was a good chance that seeing Avery Barnett, fresh from finishing her degree, back home for good, and then winning your date at the auction, could give you hope that she might have feelings for you."

"She *clearly* listened to you," I say, looking over at him now that we're on the highway.

"She did. But she may have had a thing or two to say in return."

Again, just silence. But this time I break.

"Tommy Landen, are you going to actually tell me something?"

"I had just eaten lunch with Courtney and we were talking about the whole Avery-bidding-on-you thing and she mentioned that Avery seemed to have a crush on you since high school. I wasn't surprised, because, let's be honest, what person within ten years of whatever age you are, hasn't pined for you at least a little."

I roll my eyes at him. I'm fully aware that I tend to have my pick of who I'd like to bring home on any given night, but it's just ridiculous to hear Tommy say it.

"Now, I'm not giving you all the details because there are certain things that best friends don't divulge, even to their biggest and oldest brothers."

"We both know that Bryant is bigger than me," I comment.

He ignores me. "But I will tell you this: I would have been running interference if I thought anything was going on that could hurt you," he says. "Besides Chase."

"Besides Chase."

He must be able to feel the shift in my mood because Tommy swats my arm.

"You're going to be fine, Jax. The first step is to get her back home, right? You can handle that with your eyes closed."

When did this kid get to be so sensible?

"You know that Chase is going to be there, too," I remind him.

"Yes, and that you get to be the helpful-best-friend in his eyes."

I make a non-committal sound in my throat as I let that sink in.

Maybe Wednesday won't be a disaster after all.

Chapter 13
Avery

I'm not too proud to admit finding a parking space in front of the coffee shop is much easier with Stacy's sedan. I won't tell Tommy though, he'll worry that I'm going to convert to a full city girl lifestyle.

I pull into the diagonal spot, grab my bag, and take a breath. My besties are going to have questions and I'm not sure I have answers, at least not answers that I have any confidence in.

The bell above the door jingles when I open it, drawing the eyes of everyone in the cafe. I wave to the familiar faces before I reach the counter. The only wall without doors or windows has a gorgeous mural. It feels like it captured my favorite aspects of life in Greenstone: a small farmers market, horses, cattle, and people gathered in the park. The scene is presented in vibrant colors with a setting sun. It's enough to stop someone in their tracks.

"Hey Avery, are you home for good?" Sarah, the owner, asks.

"In just a few days. The mural is incredible. Who did that?"

"Fiona Taylor. If I could marry a mural, I would marry that one." She sighs. "Unfortunately, I can't. But I get to look at it almost every day, so I'll settle for that."

"Who?" I know Caleb moved here not too long ago, but maybe he moved here with someone and Tommy didn't mention it.

"She's Mrs. Fields' niece. She grew up out of state and moved here with her daughter a few months ago. They're both absolute sweethearts."

"Oh, I had no idea."

"They've been a little overwhelmed with moving and learning how to handle their daily lives going from a two-parent to a one-parent household."

I give Sarah a questioning look.

"He's still in the picture and takes Celia every other weekend during the school year and he'll have her more in the summer. But that's about all I know. I didn't want to pry."

"Of course not," I say, fully knowing Sarah likes to gently pry, but she's always respectful of boundaries.

"Sweet tea for here today?" she asks.

"Yes, please, and a strawberry cream cheese muffin."

My eyes are drawn back to the mural, curious how someone who hasn't been here long, and who hasn't really visited in the past, captured our little town so well.

I pay as she plates a muffin and grabs my tea.

"She's by the back window," she says with a wink. "It'll be good to have you back home."

"Thanks, I'm looking forward to it." I mean every word.

Courtney is sitting at her favorite table; it's right where most people can't see her, but if she shifts a little bit, she has a view of the cafe. She stands to give me a hug and I'm careful to not spill my tea.

"You sure you don't need a hand packing today? I just have two appointments."

"I'm sure, but thank you. Today will mostly be Stacy and me going through the kitchen since that's where most of our things have commingled over the years," I say.

"Alright, you'll let me know if you change your mind, right?"

"Of course."

"Good. My first appointment is at noon tomorrow, so I can stay late."

I take the first sip of my tea. Damn, that's delicious.

"Chase is coming on Tuesday to help me do the final pack and we'll have a second truck and muscle on Wednesday to haul the boxes and drive everything to the farm."

She cocks an eyebrow, clearly picking up on my attempt to be evasive since we're in a public place, even if it's not too busy right now.

"I may have asked Tommy's oldest brother if he was available."

Courtney tries to school her features but fails miserably.

"That's awfully kind of Tommy's oldest brother to help a family friend out," she says. "Speaking of Tommy, he may have mentioned something to me at the group date last night. Something that someone may have neglected to tell me was more than a crush."

"Can I tell you I'm sorry and that it felt embarrassing to want someone for so long? Especially someone who has people practically lining up for a chance?"

"Caleb has taken the pressure off the Landen boys a little bit. Seriously, you should see when he and Matt go to the Rusty Spur...you'd think Caleb was a full-blown rock star and not a supposedly-retired rodeo champ." Courtney rolls her eyes. "But yes, I'll forgive you for not telling me it was still going on and that it might have been more intense than a school girl crush."

"Since we're here and talking about crushes that might be more, do you have any dates coming up?" I ask.

"Nope." She pops the "p" and I break off a bit of my muffin. "I might turn my profiles back on for the dating apps."

Taking my first bite, the sweetness of the strawberries hits followed by the tang of the cream cheese. It's delicious.

"Oh my God this is even more delicious than I remembered. I've been away far too long."

Courtney simply snorts and says, "Duh."

"But as of Wednesday, I'm back for good," I say, reaching my hand across the table. Courtney puts hers in mine and I give it a squeeze. "And the second you turn your apps back on I better be there with you before you swipe left OR right."

"You got yourself a deal."

Damn, I've missed all of this. Even if things don't happen with Jackson, Greenstone has everything else I'll ever need.

Courtney spills on the latest gossip at the salon and I enjoy the hour I spend with her, not realizing how tightly wound I've been with finishing up school and how much I've put on hold.

But I'll be right where I'm meant to be in a few more days, and that thought brings me peace.

And a few butterflies.

Chapter 14
Jackson

I'm wrapping the stallion's back leg and trying to not stress about moving Avery back home when I hear footsteps that are decidedly not Chet's. No, he's still on his lunch break. It's too early for Chase to stop by, so it has to be one of my brothers.

Sure enough, Chuck comes around the corner with his baseball hat on backwards, which means he's heading to the chopper.

"Heard you did well last night," he says.

Shit. Are people already talking?

"Mrs. Fields was interested in a healthy bidding war," I manage to say.

"Damn. I heard Caleb was the only one who got a higher donation."

My entire body relaxes. He's not talking about Avery and me. Whatever that might be. He's just talking about the auction itself.

"I was outside for Caleb's, but I heard he put on quite the show up there."

"Well, he already has plenty of experience working a crowd." He pauses. "Tommy seemed happy with his turn."

There's a shift in his voice.

"What?"

Chuck puts a toothpick in his mouth and chews on it for a few moments. "You can't say anything."

My eyes narrow. "What?"

"Maisy messaged him today."

He must see the shock on my face because he continues without another prompt.

"Just a little bit ago. I was able to get everything for replacing the fencing on the west end, you're welcome by the way. But I got home, showered, and went to grab something to eat before I left to see if the temporary fix was still solid enough. Anyways, he was in the kitchen, his phone chimed, and when he looked down, he looked like he saw a ghost." Chuck waits for a moment. Usually, he does it for dramatic effect, but every now and then, he's choosing his words carefully. He doesn't seem to be in cocky storyteller mode right now, which makes my hair stand on end.

"And?" I prompt, running my hands over the dressing one final time.

"He tried to hide it, but I took his phone like the nosy jackass I am and saw that she's planning to move back to Greenstone by early fall."

"Is she trying to get back together with Tommy?" I ask.

Chuck shrugs. "He snatched his phone back and locked it faster than I've ever seen him move."

"Shit."

He nods. "She doesn't do a damn thing without finding a way to end up with what she wants. And one thing she's never been fond of is being alone."

I let out a deep breath and rub my cheeks to try to process this. "What did he say?"

"Just that I couldn't tell anyone because he wasn't going to reply."

"And he thinks she's going to leave him alone? Just like that?" I gather all my things and leave the stall, running my hand along the stallion's side to let him know right where I am.

Chuck opens the gate for me. "I think he *hopes* she'll let it be and leave him alone. But I don't think he's that naive."

"Was anyone else there?"

He shakes his head. "Bryant was leaving for the stables when I got to the house and Matt was meeting Caleb in town for lunch."

"Did he say anything else?" I ask.

"No." He holds his toothpick and spins it around, watching. "He was a little panicked that I'd say something to someone."

"Well, you did." He looks guilty. "But you needed to."

Our eyes meet and he nods, like he can see the sincerity that I'm trying to convey. There may only be a handful of years between us, but I've stumbled into the role that our father had by default for better or for worse. There are days when it all feels easy, running this ranch with my brothers. It's what we were born to do and we've each carved out our own space here. But there are days like this. Days where we need someone over the age of thirty-one, someone who didn't quite have the longest marriage ever, but who made a life out of the time he got to love her. Someone who wasn't me.

But we haven't had that for years and here I am, playing the role of the father, the person who Chuck can go to without fully betraying Tommy.

"So, now what?"

"We wait," I say. "You can ask him about it and just don't tell him I know. Maybe he'll talk to Courtney and Avery."

Even though my heart pounds saying her name, I make sure my face stays neutral.

"Okay. Maybe I'll threaten to tell you all if he doesn't say something to them before she moves. Unless you think she'll drop it when he doesn't respond?"

"I'd love to have Maisy never *think* of Tommy again let alone be in contact with him. But she's nothing if not persistent. And she was long gone before she saw what it took for him to really be himself once more." My jaw muscles flex as I clench my teeth, remembering how torn apart Tommy was when she left him for another guy.

"So we pretend you don't know and I make a deal with him that I'll keep my trap shut if he tells Courtney and Avery about it before Maisy comes back."

"And we hope she finds some other guy before the end of the summer."

"Who bid on him?" Chuck asks.

"Courtney won the bid, but I couldn't see who else tried."

"Damn. If he was dating someone, she might back off."

"Do you really think Maisy would let another woman stand in the way of what she thinks she deserves?"

"No, but it was worth a shot," he says. He puts his toothpick back in his mouth before winking at me and saying, "I've got over one hundred females waiting on me, so I'd best head to the sky."

And *there's* my cocky brother.

Chapter 15
Avery

Why is moving so much work?

You'd think I'd be decent at it, or at least efficient after moving six times since graduating high school. But no. Boxing up your things, even with your brother's help for an entire day, is still a shit-ton of work. It helps that Stacy is keeping the apartment so I only have to deep clean my bedroom, really. I'm strongly considering throwing most of what I own away as I look at all of these boxes.

And then the muscle shows up, looking sexy as ever, even from the third-floor windows. I make sure I don't stare as he walks away from his SUV, or that I didn't purposefully need to "check" these boxes just to catch an early glimpse.

"Chase," I call out, hearing a non-committal response mumbled from the next room. "Will you hit the button to let Jackson in?"

"Yeah, I got his text, don't worry," he replies.

"Thanks, I'll be there in a minute."

It's a good idea to at least attempt to not blush. I'm not ashamed of what I'm wearing or anything. It's not like Jackson hasn't seen me in moving-day clothes before, but I feel like a scrub next to him. My hair is frizzy and my armpits are clearly very sweaty and from the glimpse I had of him, he's looking fine as hell.

I make my way to the main room when I hear the door open and the quiet voices of the guys greeting each other. When I walk into view they're doing the hug where they almost shake hands and then loudly pat each other's backs. But my brief view of Jackson on his way in was definitely right because he looks, well, he looks like Jackson Landen and I'd love to just eat him up. Chase turns around to grab a box and Jackson lets his gaze wander down my body with an appreciative smile on those kissable lips.

Well, that'll make a girl feel hot and bothered in a whole different way.

I'm still trying to figure out if there had been a moment where I could have kissed him on that bus but snuggling against him felt like enough of a risk. Something could have gotten back to Chase that would make him freak out before Jackson and I even had a chance to talk to him.

"Hey," he says, giving me a wink.

"Hey, thanks so much for coming," I say, trying so hard to not do anything that would tip Chase off because I just want to wrap my arms around Jackson immediately.

"Of course. I would never pass up a chance to have your oatmeal chocolate chunk cookies."

"She's leaving extra dough for Stacy, but I say we grab it before we leave," Chase fake whispers.

"You'd be the one on the losing end of Stacy's wrath. She loves those cookies, so grab her stash at your own peril," I say.

Jackson chuckles and goes to grab the next box, but I oh-so-conveniently left a heavy one in my closet.

"Actually, I have a box that I promised I wouldn't make Chase carry. It's in the closet." I make sure I sound exhausted.

Chase just peeks over his shoulder with his arms full as he heads down the hallway to the elevator, saying, "You're too kind, Jax! I saw her pack it last night and told her she'd need a linebacker for it."

"A former linebacker will have to do, I guess," Jackson says as the door closes. He follows me past Stacy's room where she waves from her computer, working on something for a potential client.

I usher Jackson into my bedroom and push the box out of the closet, which would not have been possible if we had chosen an apartment with carpet. It really is a beast of a box. And then I step right on top of it.

Jackson cracks a smile as he walks up to me and asks, "Am I carrying you *with* the box?"

"No."

"Hmmm," he hums. "I wouldn't mind it."

With my heart fluttering in my chest, I reach my hands out, grab his shirt, and bring his face right up close to mine, pausing to let him pull away if he needs to.

"I've just been dying to do this for far too long," I tell him.

I close the gap and feel his arms wrap around me, pulling me against his chest in a searing kiss that is somehow better than every single dream I've had.

Kissing Jackson Landen is better than a glass of cold lemonade on a hot summer day. His lips are pure perfection, and he knows exactly what to do with them. Before I let myself open my mouth, lord knows how badly I want to taste this man, I pull back.

There's a question in his eyes and I bite my lower lip.

"More later. It's a fast elevator and Chase will lose his shit if he thinks anything is going on."

"Right." He abruptly lets go and takes a step back.

But immediately after I step down from the box, I find his hand holding my chin, tipping my face up. His eyes are scorching as they stare into mine, and he leans down and takes a deep breath in through his nose. His jaw clenches and he oozes authority.

"More. Later." Only it practically comes out as a growl, and I let out a little whimper at what he's promising.

Why are those two words enough to make me want to lock Chase out of the whole building and damn the consequences?

He leans down even more until he nips my earlobe, causing me to gasp, before stepping around me to squat down for the box.

Damn his ass is a piece of art.

And then I notice the belt.

"You wore it again."

He turns and the box is covering the buckle itself, but I'd know the shade of leather he paired it with anywhere.

He just smirks at me before saying, "I can't imagine what you're talking about."

"Uh-huh," is all I can say as I grab two lamps and follow him down the hallway.

At least I have an excellent view when I'm behind him.

Chapter 16
Jackson

Chase and I wait as Avery does the final walk-through with Stacy. The cookies just came out of the oven and they're packed up in two containers for the ride home.

"Will you have time to stop by and see Ava after we unload the trucks? I've got a beer with your name on it."

"Of course, but only if Daffodil allows it."

"You and me both," he replies.

"Wait, she's still sitting between you two?"

"The only time she's not making contact with Ava. She's still content to sleep on the floor, but she did haul her own bed to Ava's side," he says miserably.

"Ouch."

"Yep. But she doesn't see me as the enemy, it's still more of an over-protective mother hen situation."

"Okay! We're all set." Avery comes around the corner, handing her keys to Stacy.

"Have a good drive home," she says as they hug, and we're ushered out the door and to the elevator.

"I'm picking the music," Chase says as we get in.

"Chase, as much as I love you, spending the past twenty-four hours with you is pushing our limits. I'd rather squeeze between boxes in the back of Jackson's truck than listen to what you call music."

"Well, that wasn't offensive," Chase retorts.

"You know we'll end up screaming at each other before we leave the city limits," she counters.

Chase opens his mouth to argue only to close it.

"Fair enough," he concedes.

"So I get to play DJ in the one and only Jackson Landen's truck."

"SUV," Chase corrects.

Avery just rolls her eyes and looks at me.

"What? You two don't need me for this." There's no way I'm going to willingly put myself in a Barnett sibling argument that doesn't really involve me. I'm saving everything for the battle that matters.

We get outside and I put the final box of odds-and-ends in the back before closing the trunk and getting in the driver seat.

Avery is already in the passenger seat, taking off her shoes.

"You realize that there's no way your feet smell good."

"Says the guy with four brothers who run a ranch. If my feet smell worse than what you all produce on a daily basis, I'll put my shoes back on."

What am I going to say to that? Plus, if having stinky feet in my car means she's in it, I'll take it. I think we both know it, too.

"Alright then, what are you forcing my ears to endure?" I ask, turning on the car.

She scrunches up her nose before saying, "I figured we could actually, you know, talk?"

"Probably a better idea than me having my way with you right now with Chase planning to drive behind us, wouldn't it?"

The heat in her eyes tells me I'm not the only one wanting the "more" and "later" to happen immediately.

"Just a little. But maybe we should start by pulling out of this parking spot." She puts her hand on my thigh.

"Are you trying to play with fire, Avery Barnett?" I ask, my voice dropping and becoming more authoritative.

"I already told you that I'm playing for keeps and I meant it."

I put the SUV in gear to get us on the road so Chase doesn't have a reason to be suspicious.

"Tommy has kept me updated on his life on the ranch, but what's new with you?" she asks.

"Avery Barnett, are you kicking off this mini road trip with small talk?"

"I'm trying to start a normal conversation."

I look over at her and laugh. "It's not like you don't already know exactly what's on my mind."

"I actually don't, which is why I thought we could use this time to not only be around each other but talk through some things."

"Okay then, let's talk. Why now?" I make sure she doesn't get to ask me something right off the bat.

"I'm back."

"That's not talking."

"It's more than I've ever said before. Why don't you try telling me why you're receptive to this instead?" She motions to the space between us.

"It's not like this has happened before," I remind her. "So, why now?"

"Because I'm done dating boys when I've known for far too long which man I want." She lets out a huff. "And he's not helping this conversation."

"And the ring comment?" I ask, just because I need to hear from her how serious she was with Gary.

"There was never a ring, or talk of a ring, or a hint of a ring. And we've been done for a while. That was just Tommy talking out the side of his mouth to rile you up so I could reassure you that I'm single." She rests her sock-covered feet on the dash and looks at me. "I've answered two questions now."

"Sort of."

"I did. And now I want to know why you didn't keep me at arm's length the moment I walked out back to find you at the auction."

I swallow because I've been wondering that myself.

"I should have," I say, knowing there's plenty of truth in that statement. "But I was tired."

"Tired of what? It's not like I throw myself at you often."

"You didn't throw yourself at me, trust me on that." I let out a laugh.

"Yes, please remind me of how well you know what that looks like," she said sarcastically.

"You know what they've all been," I say, and before she has time to ask what the hell I mean by that, I give her a bigger truth. "I was tired of pretending to not see you."

I look over at her and see that I definitely have her attention. I give myself a second so I can choose my words carefully. I'm not going to lie to her, but just because I figured things out, including how I feel about her, a long time ago, doesn't mean it's a good idea to dump all that on her the first time we have a real conversation.

"Growing up, I felt like a big brother to you, and don't make that face, you know exactly what I mean. But you were never Chase's annoying little sister. You were someone to look out for. So I guess as we all got older, that feeling became more of a protector where I got to secretly hate all of your boyfriends because they were never good enough for you."

"It wasn't a secret," she grumbles.

"I'll pretend I didn't hear that," I say, smirking at her before continuing. "Along the way, it went from protective to jealous. I wanted to be the one to be with you. But by the time I figured that out, I already had a bit of a reputation—"

"Just a bit," she mumbles.

"...for not being with anyone longer than a few months. When they started to get serious, I'd bail. I knew I wasn't going to return their feelings, so why prolong anything? So I started being upfront and telling anyone I was seeing that it was never going to be anything more than a few nights. And there have been very few exceptions to that."

I'm not sure what else to say and she's silent. I don't feel bad for being upfront and honest with anyone I've seen, and Avery knows my history and has never seemed to have a problem with it.

But what if she does?

Chapter 17
Avery

I don't think I've ever heard Jackson Landen be so open in my entire life.

He's not really a man of few words and he's also not a chatterbox. But he has mastered the art of easy conversation.

And he just dropped the mother-lode of why Chase has been dead set on neither Susan nor me ever thinking of Jackson in a romantic way. She moved away fast enough for Chase to not remind her weekly when she was single that there are plenty of fish in the sea and to ignore his best friend.

I feel like a shit for asking, but if we want to actually try something, we both deserve to be on the same page. "And do you, hypothetically, feel like you could *potentially* return serious feelings with someone in the future?"

I can see him swallow before looking over at me. "I think you already know that answer."

"I think we both need to hear it out loud."

He clenches his jaw for a moment and when he speaks, his voice is raw.

"No hypothetical needed." He clears his throat. "But to be clear, the answer is yes."

Before I can respond, he surprises me by asking, "And Chase?"

"I'm not going to lie and say I'm planning to have a conversation with him tonight or anything like that. No use poking the bull before knowing we're not out of our minds, right?"

"So are you wanting to test things out? Because he's going to kill me either way."

"If we're going to deal with the fallout of...not being apart, then I think that would make sense. Having some expectations or rules."

"Like not telling Chase for a set amount of time," he states.

"That could be the first rule. How about no hints in public that we're trying things out?"

There's a moment of silence.

"Are you *trying things out* with other people or just with me?" He gets a possessive heat in his eyes, and I definitely squeeze my thighs together.

"What I said before about my dating history still stands: I know what I want and I'm not interested in anything else. So no," I say before adding, "and you?"

"The second your lips touched mine I knew I wasn't going to kiss anyone else."

Damn. There was zero hesitation there.

Until just now, I didn't realize I was worried about Jackson not wanting to be exclusive. Since he hasn't *really* dated that much, there wasn't much time for him to be monogamous over the years.

"Well, okay then." I look out the window to hide my smile and my furiously blushing face.

We drift into a period of easy silence before he switches on some music. He keeps the volume low, so we can still talk.

"If you want to listen to something else, you can change it."

"I think this is nice," I reply, tipping my head back and letting my eyes fall shut. I hear him shift a little and his fingers interlock with mine. Butterflies flutter in my stomach like I'm back in high school and his calloused palm makes me feel grounded. I can't believe I waited this long to say something. I let myself fully relax against the seat, feeling the sun on my face and just how tired I am.

I wake with a small start, my hand still engulfed by Jackson's. Without turning his head, his smirk grows and he peeks at me.

"How long was I out?" I ask, stretching out my back.

"We're not too far from Greenstone, actually."

"We are not!" I grab my phone, open my map app, and my eyes widen.

"I mean, you defended your thesis, spent a weekend in Greenstone, and then packed up your apartment with Chase. I can't imagine you've gotten a lot of sleep."

"But I *fell asleep* during our car ride where we were going to talk!" Oh this is mortifying.

"You felt comfortable enough to relax and get what you need," he says. "I took it as a compliment."

How do you stay embarrassed after he says that?

"Let's pretend that I was stressed out and stayed awake and make the most out of the rest of our drive," I suggest.

"Okay, how do we arrange for *more*?" He raises his eyebrow at me. God, he's one sexy man. "I'm afraid that I'm not going to be very good at being patient."

"We need to do things away from Chase and other prying eyes while we test the waters."

"Baby, I'm not testing any waters, I'm diving right in." He tightens his grip on the steering wheel while I try to keep my hands to myself. That nickname is going to be the death of my restraint.

"Oh boy, you're not helping plan the logistics."

"It's not my fault that I just want your mouth on mine."

That switches the gears in my head.

"I have other ideas for my mouth, but I want to have some sort of game plan before we leave this enclosed space away from Chase."

Chapter 18
Jackson

Just when I think she's already too perfect, she goes and says something like that.

Fuck, I have imagined places where that mouth of hers could go...

"Game plan: I get you alone at least three times a day to have my way with you, preferably in places where you can scream as loud as you need."

"Cocky much?" she says while physically squirming.

"Just telling you exactly what I want while we have to be quiet about things." I swear she melts just a little more into the seat.

"You're not being helpful, Jackson."

"Fine." I consider a compromise. "I get you for at least one hour every day."

"What? How the hell is that *not* going to be suspicious?" she sputters.

"It'll be less suspicious than me losing my patience and hauling you over my shoulder while you're at the Barnett dinner table."

"Jesus Christ, Jackson, I'm trying to think of something *helpful* that won't end your friendship with my brother."

I clench my jaw, hating Chase at this moment. I've never blamed him for his one rule. And until this past week, I was ready to follow it forever.

"Tommy and Misty," I say matter-of-factly.

"Huh?"

"You'll get back into regularly riding Misty a few days a week, and then we'll ask Tommy to be home on certain nights. You can park at his place, and I'll pick you up and bring you to mine."

"That's not a terrible idea," she says.

"I am nothing if not determined when I want something."

"You know that Tommy will be pissed if I never actually spend time with him," she notes.

"This is a temporary solution while we figure things out. I'm not spending the rest of my life not being able to grab your ass in public."

"I never took you for an ass-grabbing kind of guy, Jackson."

"I never had access to my favorite one."

She blushes furiously.

"Okay, so when do we tell Chase?" she asks.

I pause. I know how I feel about her. I'll put up with snoring, smelly-ass feet, temper-tantrums, and her shit all over the place if it means I wake up with the woman of my dreams in my arms. But one thing at a time.

"We know that he'll need to be eased into the idea without being tipped off. And if you or I hint at anything, he'll likely jump down our throats before we can say more than two words."

"I'll talk to Ava and see if she can start buttering him up without putting him on the defensive. I don't have to tell her anything about us, just see if she'll encourage him to see that we're adults and he should get off our backs after all these years. And we can hang out as friends in public just fine. He doesn't say much when other people are around."

"You can't give me any looks."

"I'd never!"

"You have been."

She holds up one finger and says, "Not when he's around," and the second one comes up, "and only because I won a date with you. Also, Tommy may have mentioned that you might need to be hit over the head with a two-by-four in order to take the hint."

"He wasn't wrong," I chuckle.

"No, he wasn't. I could practically hear the gears turning in your head that evening before we got to the park."

I switch hands on the steering wheel so I can hold my right one out to her.

"So we're doing this?" I ask.

"We're doing this," she replies, putting her hand in mine.

She turns and looks out her window behind us, checking the side and rear-view mirrors from a few angles.

"What are you doing?" I ask.

"Just making sure Chase won't notice if I duck out of view for a little bit."

"What?"

"Remember, I had something I wanted to do with my mouth during this car ride?" She bats her eyes at me before saying, "And I've been wanting to get a closer look at that belt buckle I had made for you last year. It took forever for the artist to get it right."

"I thought you said you had it done on a random website," I remark, trying to ignore how hard my dick is at what she's implying.

She slips the shoulder part of the seat belt behind her so she can lean forward.

"You can keep us from crashing, right?"

"Are you questioning my ability to multitask for the few minutes we have left before we get to town?"

"No." She puts her hand on the buckle. "Would you like to not have me..."

She tips her head toward my crotch.

"Only a fool would say no to those lips, Avery."

She pops the buckle and loosens the belt.

"You're going to stay low enough so your brother doesn't see you bobbing up every now and then?"

"As long as you keep your ass on the seat and he doesn't decide to pass us, we should be fine."

"Deal."

She undoes the button and unzips my fly and the faint smell of her peach shampoo hits me, driving me wild.

"May I?"

"Only if you're ready to suck down every last drop."

My hand is already on the back of her head when she frees my shaft.

"Yes, please," she breathes out.

"That's my girl."

Chapter 19
Avery

Okay, I've never liked going down on my exes but holy fuck I want to go down on this man daily before he sinks this glorious dick deep inside of me. Just thinking about him on top of me has me moaning.

"Jesus, Avery."

I tongue down his shaft, tracing his big vein with my lips before swirling my tongue around the tip, causing Jackson to grunt.

Fisting the base of his dick, I pump while adding more saliva so my hand can slide better. His fingers are working my ponytail loose so he can grip my hair. "That's it, your mouth fits me so perfectly–"

I suck hard, increasing the pressure from my fingers, cutting off whatever he was going to say next with a sharp inhale. If I could smirk right now, I would.

I'm not naive. I know Jackson Landen has been with half the damn town. But being able to feel him react to me like this? I'll have to make sure I don't get an ego because he is hard as a rock and when I flick my tongue against the ridge of his head, everything twitches.

"Fuck yes, Avery, just like that."

He adds some pressure to the back of my head and I take more of him into my mouth, bobbing up and down with my tongue flicking from one side of his shaft to the other. I can feel his whole body reacting now—his legs trying to stay still and his back arching to offset his reflex to rock his hips forward.

I hear him groan in frustration. "Baby I promise we'll have time to do so much more of this, but we just passed the turnoff to my place." His breath hitches as I make a disappointed sound around his dick, clearly loving the vibrations it causes. "So, now's the time to take everything you can."

Determined to taste every last drop of Jackson, I will my gag reflex to relax and take him as deep as possible until I feel him hit the back of my throat.

"Such a good fucking girl," he says.

I would smack anyone else for calling me a good girl, but when it's coming from Jackson Landen's mouth, I'm an absolute mess of desire. I hold my head in one spot because he's gyrating his hips to hit the angles he needs.

"Suck hard once more, baby." It's a cross between a request and a demand.

I drop my face down lower and do as he asks right before he grunts and starts coming down my throat. I pull back just enough to give me space to swallow as my mouth continues to hold the suction, working him until he starts to jerk and his hand releases my hair.

Leaning back to get a good look, I see that his entire dick is glistening from my ministrations, but his jeans seem dry. Which means, thankfully, there's no evidence for anyone else to find.

I move my head out of his lap, wiping my mouth and chin while keeping low so Chase doesn't notice me through the side mirror on Jackson's side. The back of the SUV is so full, Chase wouldn't be able to see if I started doing a striptease in the passenger seat.

Sitting up, I look over at Jackson, who is already getting himself back into his pants with one hand, which is oddly erotic to watch.

"Are you kidding me?" Jackson asks, drawing my attention back to his eyes, which are glued to my face.

"What?"

"How the fuck am I supposed to keep my hands off you when you look like that?" he groans and gestures towards my face.

I tip the visor down to flip open the mirror.

Well, shit. I didn't think about the fact that I might be a *bit* disheveled after going down on the guy of my dreams. I'm totally flushed, too, and we only have another minute before we reach the main house.

"Tell me things that *aren't* sexy," I say, trying not to panic and making my blush worse.

"What?"

"Things that aren't sexy! You need to un-turn me on before anyone sees this hot mess." I flap my hand in front of my face.

He has the audacity to chuckle at me while rubbing a hand on the back of his neck, making him look even sexier.

"That's not a real phrase."

I swat him. "Stop that."

"Stop what?" he asks.

"Just...stop moving."

"Because any movement I make isn't working to un-turn you on?" He waggles his eyebrows at me and, of course, it's not ridiculous...it's sexy.

I let out a dramatic sigh and crank the A/C, putting my face directly in front of the closest vent and yanking my hair back into a non-manhandled mess.

Chapter 20
Jackson

I've had plenty of women and men go down on me, and I returned the favor each time, but not one of them got me off as fast as Avery Barnett. Granted, the clock was definitely ticking, but there wasn't much needed to speed things along.

And her face after...I almost pulled over, laid my seat all the way back, and pulled her up so she was fully sitting on my mouth with her shorts and underwear anywhere but between my tongue and her—

"Earth to Jax." Chase waves his free hand in front of my face, bringing me back to my current reality.

"Sorry, I should've had a coffee on the drive home and not the cookies," I say, knowing that anything has to be better than saying I was daydreaming about eating out his sister who just gave me the best fucking head of my life.

"As long as you can carry that end of the headboard up to Avery's room, we'll be fine."

I pick up my end and think of the epic blanket Mrs. Fields crocheted for the auction instead of letting my mind wander to what Avery would look like holding the top of the headboard as I pound into her from behind. *Large, brown blankets made from yarn that's never actually soft. Large, brown blankets...*

We make our way up the wide staircase of the main house with the headboard, giving a view of their entryway and part of the huge kitchen. I've spent so much time in this house, but it's different heading into Avery's childhood bedroom. Their parents already moved the twin bed out so her regular bed could be moved in now that she's back for good. My already-possessive heart gives a few satisfied thumps at the thought of it being me who is going to put this bed together.

I don't care who's been in it before, I just know I'm the only one who gets to hold her in it from now on. Not that I'm going to stay at her parents' house any time soon...but one day we might spend a holiday here.

We set the headboard down and get to work putting the frame together when Chase sighs and I already know what's coming.

"Look, Jax. I know I sound like a complete dick of a best friend, but since she's back—just hear me out—I just need to know that Avery isn't a target for being another notch on your bedpost."

"Jesus, Chase, are you fucking serious?" I didn't even hear Avery come back to the doorway and she's fully geared up for a fight. "I'm a grown-ass woman and if I want to be someone's bedpost notch, I'll do as I damn well please."

"You absolutely will n—"

"Do *not* finish that thought out loud, Chase Martin Barnett," she warns. "I may be five years younger than you..."

"Almost six," he gripes.

She lets out an exasperated sound. "But I'm an adult and my sex life is *none* of your concern. Jackson is an adult. Tommy is an adult. Ava is an adult."

"Don't bring my pregnant wife into this conversation."

"I'm making a point, you jackass. You haven't pulled this shit with Susan since she started dating Christopher, but everyone else, including me, became an adult a long time ago and you have *got* to stop policing us just because we're single. Do you think Jackson and I don't know about each other's dating histories?"

I hold my breath because this is *not* how things were supposed to go. But, thankfully, she's on a roll. Hell, we might not need to have to chat with Ava about getting Chase off our backs.

"Do you think that Bryant doesn't have his scars? What about Susan? Just because she's married and has two kids already doesn't mean that she doesn't have a major red flag or two." She takes a breath. "So, for the love of all that is holy, back the fuck off and let the adults be adults. And before you go on a crusade, *no*, I'm not looking to be a notch on Jackson's bedpost. Who uses that phrase anymore? Does anyone actually carve notches on their bedpost when they—"

"Stop. I'm not talking about bedpost notches with my baby sister." Chase works his jaw, clearly trying to not look like an ass but wanting to say a whole lot. He lets out a sharp exhale through his nose. "I just can't handle seeing your heart broken again."

Avery visibly softens. "I appreciate that, Chase, I really do. But part of letting someone in means that you risk your heart being broken. And seventeen-year-old-Avery is very different from who I am now. You aren't responsible for what I do with my heart. I've made stupid decisions in the past, but I'm still here."

"It's never going to come naturally for me to not look out for you," he says.

"I know, and don't think I never noticed how much you stepped up when Mom and Dad were separated. Susan saw it, too. But I don't need a protector." She picks at the hem of her t-shirt. "I just need you to be my brother."

I can't tell if Chase nods because he doesn't want the lecture from his youngest sibling drawn out longer, or if something she said actually sunk in.

But he looks at me and I know it's the former.

Chapter 21
Avery

If I stay any longer, any grateful feelings, however messed up, will go out the window and I'll lose my shit. I turn around and head down to the kitchen, feeling right at home with the granite countertops and antler chandelier.

Is there a rule book for helicopter brothers who are an almost-constant cock block? Because hearing Chase tell Jackson to steer clear of me made me want to throttle him, which is frowned upon in most households.

My heart ached seeing Jackson's face right before I announced my presence. He's not some timid little puppy, he's more like a quiet stud horse, but when Chase started to tell him to stay away from me, he looked defeated. I can only imagine what he's heard from my brother over the years, especially before Susan started seeing Christopher and Chase was on a mission to keep *both* Barnett girls immune to the oldest Landen brother's charms.

As I fill a glass with water, I hear the front door close thanks to its over-zealous spring. I'd know the sound of those boots anywhere and turn to see the soft smile of my mom with her arms outstretched.

"I'm so happy you're officially back," she says, pulling me in for a hug. "What can I do?"

"You literally just walked in the door from your three-day conference, there's nothing for you to handle. But thank you," I tell her. "Plus, the heavy lifting has been handled."

"Was Tommy able to get out of his presentation?" she asks.

"No, Jackson's upstairs with Chase right now putting the bed together." I hate that I need to be so casual every time I say Jackson's name out loud.

I guess knowing we have a plan makes things a little easier than just pretending to have zero interest in the county's most gorgeous bachelor. Trying things out privately to make sure we actually like being around each other, when we've avoided it for so long, is the smart thing to do. The right thing to do. If we wanted to be together in public from the start and we somehow weren't compatible? Chase would flip his lid immediately and nothing good can come from something with that much pain. And I do mean pain because there's no way he wouldn't lash out at being blindsided by his sister and best friend being together.

"Oh perfect," she says. "One of the speakers was a new large animal vet who is just finishing up a long-term study on the potential benefits of ranches and farms having both chickens and horses. It was fascinating."

"And Jackson is a candidate for receiving chickens to buddy-up with his horses?" I ask, so confused.

"No, well, he actually does have a lot of potential for having a chicken roost close to the stables near his house, just not fully living together because horses can't digest chicken poop. What I was thinking though, is that Dr. Rebecca is looking for a place to put down roots."

My stomach drops. Is she trying to set Jackson up with this chicken lady?

She must sense confusion coming from me because she says, "Jackson is the one who had the idea for the fundraiser and who did the research for purchasing the equipment. I was thinking that he might be able to talk to Dr. Rebecca about what the town did and what it might have to offer for potential clients."

I'm about to say that Sam handles the purchases and I can't believe that statement almost came out of my mouth. I very nearly referred someone to Samantha Davies over Jackson. All because of what? Jealousy? It's not like Jackson would meet a vet and gallop off with her into the sunset.

"That's a great idea," I manage to say. "If you have her info, you can give it to him before he leaves with Chase to see Ava."

"Here, I'll send it to you to pass along, I'm going to unpack since you three have things handled."

She heads out as my phone dings with the contact information for one Rebecca Quist. Well, if I'm going to give my secret boyfriend some other woman's number, I might as well remind him I make his favorite cookies...

Chapter 22
Jackson

Chase and I are securing the last bolts of Avery's bed when she comes around the corner with two glasses of milk and a pile of oatmeal chocolate chunk cookies. Damn, she looks amazing.

Don't gawk, I remind myself.

"Mom's back," she tells Chase before looking at me. "And I have something for you."

It takes just about everything I have to not stare at her, or to look at Chase, or panic. She sets down the plate of cookies and hands each of us a glass of milk.

"Get your phone out so I can share something with you," she says, pulling hers out of her pocket, drawing my eyes to her hips.

Thankfully, Chase is busy dunking his first cookie as I grab my phone.

"Here's the info for Rebecca Quist," she says.

Wait, what?

"You need to reach out to her," she continues as if it's perfectly normal to have the guy you're secretly seeing call some other woman. "She's a large animal vet who might be ready to move. My mom met her at the conference and thought you could tell her about the equipment being purchased from the fundraiser, since you were the one who did all the research. She apparently knows a lot about horses and chickens."

She gives me a knowing smile as she digs into the cookies. I suppose her giving me another woman's number is one way to keep Chase unaware.

"Do I have to call or can I text?" I ask, attempting to act like any of this is normal.

"You should eventually have an actual conversation with her, but you can warm up to it by texting," she says with a smirk.

We finish off the plate of cookies, and the three of us go downstairs, something that I've done a million times, just not always with Avery in the mix. Chase heads off to the right to say hi to their mom who's still unpacking, leaving me alone with Avery.

The second he's out of sight, I pull her tight against me so I can feel all of her curves.

"You meant it when you said you weren't going to have any patience, didn't you?" she asks, automatically wrapping her arms around my waist.

"Absolutely," I say before tilting her chin up and swooping down for a quick kiss, breathing in her peach scent. I'm never going to get tired of those lips, or that smell.

I take a step back and motion for her to lead the way out the front door. Right after she turns around, I do what I've been dreaming about for way too long.

I grab her ass, making her squeal and me groan. Jesus, like everything about Avery Barnett, it's even better than I've imagined.

"When do I get you alone?" I ask, crowding behind her when we're on the open front porch, savoring the last few moments of privacy with the breeze blowing through her hair.

"I'll stop by to ride Misty after dinner," she says, leaning against me.

"It's like you knew I'd be needing dessert tonight," I whisper as I run my hand around her hip, tracing the small ridge her underwear makes. "I can't tell you how much I'm looking forward to finally tasting you."

She takes a sharp inhale and before I get carried away, I step around her, letting my fingers trail a little lower as I pass. She lets out a whimper.

"Don't be late," I call from the sidewalk.

"Late for what?" Chase's voice is coming from the kitchen, so I know he didn't see, or hear, anything else.

As he comes out to the porch, I look up at my best friend with a twinge of guilt.

"She's going to stop by and take Misty for a ride before it gets dark," I reply, trying to sound natural.

Chase mock-glares at Avery. "Don't give her any treats to butter her up."

"Yeah, yeah, no one can replace her Sugar Daddy, Chase. We know." She rolls her eyes before sitting in one of the rocking chairs with her feet on the railing. "Tell Ava to come up for dinner if she's not sick."

"She was feeling better when I called on the drive home, so we might be able to join everyone tonight. Must be the shift to the second trimester."

"Good. Thanks, again, you two. I owe you both." Avery tips her head back and closes her eyes as Chase and I walk down the path to his place.

My gut feels heavy. I've walked every inch of this property and it's a second home to me, but now I'm next to Chase and I know I'm going to hurt him. It doesn't matter that Avery is the only person I've ever loved. We just need to find a way to tell him that won't cause him to shut us out without hearing what we have to say.

I think back to college when Chase found out that our roommate Jerry had a one-night-stand with Susan. She was devastated when she found out it wasn't anything more and Chase punched Jerry once. But it was so hard that they both needed stitches. Jerry's cheek was cut deep, and Chase's knuckles were split open.

Chase moved home for the rest of the semester and hasn't spoken to Jerry since.

I glance over at my best friend, determined to do this right.

Chapter 23
Avery

I enjoy the view of Jackson's backside as they head to see Ava. He's absolutely gorgeous from head to toe and I'm crawling out of my skin to get him alone this evening. I know we have things to figure out, but I think it's safe to say we're both ready to make up for lost time.

I let myself relax into the chair. God, it feels so good to be out of the city. After the chaos of finishing and defending my thesis, I've been craving the peace of rural life. I can hear birds chirping and the breeze moving the tall grasses we keep on the side of our house. The air smells clean here. Actually, I even prefer the smell here when it's time to fertilize the fields over the smells of the city.

There's rustling from the kitchen, so I leave the comfort of my rocking chair to see what Mom's up to. I slow the screen door with my foot so it doesn't slam, but the familiar creaking sound it makes confirms I'm finally back.

"You didn't go see Ava?" she asks.

"No, I thought I'd give the boys some time with her and Daffodil since she's probably coming over for dinner." I smile at how normal it feels to be around for dinner with Ava and Chase. I've been away at college for most of their relationship, but I love her like a sister and it's nice to know I'm in Greenstone for good.

"Neither of them mentioned anything about that," she huffs with a frown. "I would have picked up something that would be easy on her. She sounded a little tired on the phone."

"She's feeling pretty normal, Mom, but why don't we just do soup to keep it simple? I can grab some veggies from the garden," I offer.

"No, no. You go get settled in. I'll handle the dinner. Soup sounds delicious, actually," she says as she kisses the top of my head. "What'd you think of the new space?"

"I mean, I wouldn't call it new, but I'm already in love with not sleeping on the twin bed anymore."

"No, I meant your office," she says.

"What are you talking about? I haven't set anything up yet."

"Ah, of course he didn't say anything." She sighs and rolls her eyes. "Even if none of you look like me, at least I can say that all of my children inherited my stubbornness."

"What?"

"Go look in Chase's room," she calls as she grabs her favorite basket on her way out the door.

Confused, I head upstairs.

The door to Chase's childhood room is open and the first thing I notice is a new desk under the window. It's beautiful in its simplicity and the wood has been stained a dark auburn, bringing out the designs in the grain. There's a cup with pens, pencils, and markers next to an adjustable stand for my laptop so I can sit or stand.

There's a note on white paper from the printer on the far side of the desk, folded in half. I open it to see Chase's familiar handwriting:

I know you like your chair, so I assumed you'd want that and not something different, but you need a good desk.

I'm proud of you, sis.

-Chase

Of course that's his note. I read it a second time before chuckling and shaking my head.

I look out the window, seeing our farm stretch out into the distance. The view is close to what I grew up with except I can see the path that leads to the carriage house that Chase and Ava converted into their home. It's nice to have him so close, even though he's already as paranoid as can be.

Turning around, I see his cowboy clock is still on the wall, ticking away, but something huge catches my attention. With my back to the desk, I walk up to a gigantic map of the county, but instead of the regular map you'd find online or on your phone, it's the plots of land. Each border is thickly marked, and every property seems to be shaded a different color. I reach up and trace our farm before letting my finger follow the borderlines until they're outlining Landen Acres, in particular the northwest corner where their smaller horse stable sits along with a certain brother's house. There's a smaller poster with the key so there aren't labels on the map itself, just the topography and borders. I find a sticky note at the bottom of the key that simply says:

Open the big drawer.

Giving the hand-shaded map one more look, I head back to the desk, pulling the handle on the largest drawer on the right side. As it opens, I reveal a series of binders, each one matching the color of a property on the map. I grab the one that matches Landen Acres and smile when I see their logo on the cover. Hopping up on my new desk, I open it to the first page. There are tabs for different topics—herd, crop, services, history, notes—and the front page has an overview including the owner, family, date established, lot size, main herd/crop type, and more.

I can feel my eyes watering.

This is Chase to a T. It seems like everything goes in one ear and right out the other, but really, he's listening and cataloging things away to do something epic while barely taking credit for it. He might be a braggart for some things, but the things where he shows his love? Those are the quiet actions he does when no one's looking. The ones that take hours upon hours of work without you even knowing.

I can smell onions and garlic cooking, which means the soup has begun. If I can get cleaned up fast, I can get a flatbread in the oven so it's ready for dinner. That feels like a tiny step towards showing him I appreciate all of this, right?

Time to make sure I don't smell like a pigsty before wrapping my legs around Jackson after a family dinner.

Chapter 24
Jackson

We can hear Daffodil well before the house is in view.

"Damn, I see your dog is on full alert now, isn't she?"

"Absolutely," Chase says with a snort.

There's a pause and I know what's coming before Chase stops walking.

"Look, man. I'm sorry. I know you must think I'm the world's biggest fucking jackass for bringing up Avery and asking you to stay away from her other than being friends." He sighs and even though I absolutely hate having to listen to this again, if I suddenly push back, he'll be on the lookout for anything suspicious.

"I just—" he says, closing his eyes and letting out a long breath. "I just know how things end. She doesn't do casual, and that's what you have to offer. I didn't mean to be suddenly weird or overbearing. She's home now though and, like she reminded me, she's not seventeen. But she can still get her heart broken. And I don't know what I'd do without my best friend if that happened."

I unclench my jaw, look him right in the eye, and say the only thing that isn't a lie, "I know."

He nods and we start walking once more. My stomach feels like it has a brick in it. If she had been anyone else, I could have told him years ago. He would have understood, even with the age difference. I know he would have. But I've been telling him since we were finishing college that I wouldn't touch either of his sisters. I had no idea what would happen back then. I've meant those words. Heck, even the last time he said something, when Avery was home around my thirtieth birthday, I told him, in all honesty, that he had nothing to worry about. I knew how I felt, but I respected his one request, mainly because I didn't think there was a chance that she had anything other than friendship feelings towards me. I sure as hell wasn't going to approach her and I never saw *this* coming. Never in a million years did I think I'd have a chance of being with the woman I've wanted in silence. I dreamed about it, but that was it.

Now that I have her, I'm never letting go. I just need to find a way to show Chase the truth.

I see Ava as we come around the bend. She's sitting on their patio in a padded chair with her bulldog standing at attention with her ears perked. She waves at us and walks towards us with Daffodil right at her side.

"Hey babe," she says as Chase gives her a hug and kisses her right on the mouth, causing Daffodil to push herself between their legs and sit on his feet.

I snort, I can't help it.

After Chase and Ava step apart, I hold up my hand and say, "Hey girl," and Daffodil comes up and gives my fingers a sniff and a lick before quickly heading back with Ava.

"So Jax, did Sue tell you about the new vet?"

"Damn, news sure travels fast," Chase says.

"She called me to see if I needed anything as she was driving through town," Ava explains.

"Yeah," I say. "Avery gave me her number, so I'll text her after we're done."

"Sue might have mentioned that she's quite cute," Ava says casually.

Chase smiles. "I could see Jax settling down with a lady vet. Especially with how well you do with troublesome horses. Almost sounds like a match made in heaven."

I do my best not to growl, or say that I'm off the market, or anything boneheaded at this point.

"We'll have to see," I say. "Who knows? Maybe she'll go for the beefiest Landen brother instead? He's the better listener."

"That's because Bryant barely speaks. Especially around any potential partner," Ava says.

I just shrug. She's not wrong about that.

I know this is going to be hard, but did people have to start playing matchmaker within hours of me finally kissing the person of my dreams?

As we reach the patio, Ava has two beers waiting for us. I grab the seat that's not under the umbrella to give myself a little space from any potential scrutiny.

"You look like you're feeling a lot better than you were the last time I was here," I tell Ava.

"I swear, hitting the second trimester was like a magical switch flipped. Now I can not only smell food cooking without vomiting, I can even eat it! I have to say, I might not be the most patient pregnant person on the planet when I can't snack."

"You're way more patient than me when I'm hangry," Chase says, frowning.

"Honey, I chose my words carefully when I said 'pregnant' because everyone knows how you are when you get hangry," she says. Then she looks over at me. "Chase mentioned you have a horse coming to you on Friday. Is there anything I can do to help?"

"Thank you, but no. This one is supposed to have a bunch of seemingly little triggers for her to kick, so I wouldn't want to risk you or the baby. Bryant or Tommy will be my second set of hands to keep her calm while I get her settled in and looked over," I tell her.

"Well, she's going to be in amazing hands with you, Jax. If you do need something, even dinner prepped, I'd love to have something to occupy me so I'm not looking up every tiny thing that happens to my body."

"As long as your doctor is fine with it, I'm sure Chuck would love some company when he's in the chopper. He's going to fly over the perimeter in a few days, so you'd get some good views."

"That sounds heavenly," she moans.

"Excellent, just let us know when you have the all-clear."

Chapter 25
Avery

Poking the dough down with my fingertips is so satisfying, especially when I get the rows nice and even as I make it fill the rectangular pan. I brush the top with olive oil and then sprinkle on salt and rosemary before popping it into the oven.

My phone vibrates in my pocket, making my heart flutter. I check the screen and it's a message from Tommy. I don't let myself deflate just because I might have secretly hoped it was from an older Landen brother. But that's just silly. Jackson and I agreed to not message so we don't inadvertently out that we're testing the waters.

Or diving right in.

I shiver as I remember the confidence he had and how sure he sounded. Bringing myself back to reality, especially since I only have about fifteen minutes before I need to check the bread, I look at the message.

Tommy: Happy to have you back

A smile spreads across my face and I shoot him a quick response as I go upstairs to my bedroom. Opening one of my bathroom boxes, I grab my favorite shampoo and conditioner, it has a Georgia peach scent that I love, and a few other bottles until my arms are full. If I wasn't going to see Jackson tonight, I wouldn't be rushing to shower, but I'd rather not smell like I spent the last twenty-four hours packing up my life and moving it a few hours away.

In near record time, I'm clean, my hair is brushed and wrapped in a towel, and I'm tugging one of my dresses over my head.

I purse my lips as I consider that I'm technically going to Landen Acres to take Misty out for a ride. I decide on stuffing a pair of riding pants into my bag. If anyone asks, or anyone sees me on Misty, I won't look Iike I'm actively trying to chafe my inner thighs.

The smell of the bread greets me as I skip down the stairs. Mom and Dad are in the kitchen and Chase and Ava are setting the table.

"I didn't hear any of you come in!"

Dad gives me a big bear hug and then holds me at arm's length. "You look awfully dressed up for dinner."

Instead of panicking, I tell him a partial truth. "I needed to not feel disgusting after hauling boxes."

Chase laughs. "It's not like you did most of the hauling. You might have had help."

"I did. And I'm wildly grateful to both of you for lugging my worldly possessions back to Barnett Farms."

Ava pulls me into a hug, "We'll have to have a girls night soon."

"Definitely."

I take Chase by surprise, engulfing him in a tight hug. "Thank you," I say, my face buried in his chest.

"Whoa there, you already made me cookies," he says.

I just squeeze him tighter. "Thank you for the office."

With that, his arms wrap around me and his cheek rests against the top of my head. "Any time."

I nod against him and release him.

Mom gets everyone a generous helping of soup as I check the bread. When the oven is open, I hear everyone let out sounds of appreciation. I don't blame them. It smells divine and the crust is perfectly golden brown. I close the oven for a moment to grab the thick wooden cutting board that Chase made way back in high school. The wood is a dark walnut and the finish reminds me of the desk upstairs.

"Avery?" I look up to see Mom staring at me, a puzzled look on her face. "Is something wrong?"

"What do you mean?"

"You're staring at the cutting board like you're upset with it, or like it might bite you."

Shaking my head, I say, "No, not upset with an inanimate object. Just noticing that there are solid similarities between this and the desk in Chase's old room."

She smiles at me. "Your brother was pretty hush-hush about what he did. I don't know if he put the desk together, or if he built one himself. Either way, I'm not sure you'll get a clear answer from him."

"No, if I ask, he'd just say something like 'does it matter?' And then we'd bicker."

"I would tell you to ask Ava, but he wouldn't have worked on a desk in the house or even in the garage with her nausea and the fumes. So if he crafted it himself, he was likely alone in the process."

"You two coming?" Dad calls out.

"Crap," I mumble, opening the oven once more. Everything is okay, the top crust is just a little darker than golden brown when I turn it out of the pan and onto the cutting board.

"I think the smell of this bread alone could have cured my morning sickness, you should have moved back at least two months ago," Ava says as Chase puts his arm around her at the table.

"We should have invited Jax to join us," Dad says, making my heart pound. "Especially after everything he did today."

"Avery made oatmeal chocolate chunk cookies for us," Chase says with a mouthful of soup.

Dad stares at us. "And where are the leftovers?"

"I'll take the full blame for that," Ava says. "Chase knew I was feeling better so everything that didn't go home with Jackson was a delightful surprise for me when they came back."

Chase blushes. He never knows what to do when someone acknowledges his thoughtfulness.

"There's dough in the freezer, too," I remind him. "I made some on Sunday."

"There *was* dough in the freezer," Mom chimes in, looking pointedly at Dad. "Until someone burned the first batch to a crisp."

"But the second batch was perfection," he says, smiling at me.

This is so much better than takeout while cramming one last study session in before finals. Damn, it's good to be back.

Chapter 26
Jackson

Bryant walks in with the platter piled high with steak.

"He wasn't eaten by rabid wolves!"

"Shut up, Chuck," Bryant grumbles.

"They look amazing," Tommy says, glaring at Chuck.

"I was genuinely worried that we might have lost the muscle of the family," Chuck says with his hands up in surrender.

Bryant sets the pile of pure protein in the middle of the table and smacks the back of Chuck's head as he walks by, which just makes Chuck laugh.

Matt lifts the cover off the twice-baked potatoes and starts passing things around as I take a sip of my beer.

"What'd I miss today?" I ask.

No surprise, it's Chuck who speaks first. "The fence on the west end has more damage than we originally thought, but it's nothing that we can't tackle ourselves."

"And the cows?"

"They're grazing far enough away right now that I'm comfortable with the temporary fix we have in place and we have Shane's brother out there with him, the one finishing high school this year, so there's an extra set of eyes on everything."

I nod. "Any change in the expense of the fix?"

He shrugs. "Not really. A few hundred more at most."

I know Bryant doesn't like to go first and he hates knowing he'll have people looking at him, even if it's just us, so I always try to get to him second or third.

"Horses?" I ask.

"They're looking good. We made good progress on training one of the more headstrong stallions and he's going to be one hell of a force to be reckoned with if we can get him on the circuit with the right rider." Bryant casts a glance at Matt.

"I'm not *that* good."

Bryant rolls his eyes. "Not you. Caleb."

"He rode broncos and is still recovering from his injury," Matt says.

Bryant shrugs. "Can't hurt to see if he'd like to. I've never seen anyone stay on a horse like him."

I nod in agreement, thinking back on that rodeo five years ago with Avery and Courtney. I look at the clock, she'll be here in another twenty minutes or so and I have to fight the smile that's threatening to emerge.

Clearing my throat, I refocus on the conversation at hand. "Matt?"

"One of the new guys for this season took a hoof to the shoulder, but he was standing far enough back so it'll just be sore for a few days with a bruise and not shattered. He's good to stay on and is a solid hand. I was there when it happened and any one of us would have been kicked."

"And why are you wearing that?" I nod to his clean flannel shirt that's tucked into jeans that aren't half-covered in muck like Bryant and Chuck. "Have someplace you're heading off to?"

"Just grabbing a drink with Caleb," he says.

"He settling into life in Greenstone?" Tommy asks.

"Yeah, I guess so," Matt says. "He says he doesn't need to work, so he's focusing on himself. I think that just means he's attempting to not die of boredom after being on the circuit for so long. Plus, he's a terrible cook, so I'm going to teach him a few things. I stopped by to play video games and he had the nastiest soup, if you can call it that, on the stove and there's no way it was edible."

"Sounds like he picked the right town to settle down in," Tommy says.

"You make it sound like he's planning to get married and have kids," Matt laughs.

"Nothing wrong with that," Bryant says, making us all stare at him, mouths open.

"Did we miss something?" I ask Bryant before Chuck can come in with some sarcastic comment.

Bryant blushes but puts on a look of mild disgust and shakes his head. I kick Chuck under the table when I see him open his mouth and send him a warning glare. Bryant hasn't had a serious relationship for years. If he's actually thinking about being with someone, giving him shit right now is just going to close him up tight like a clam.

I can't think of what to say that won't likely embarrass Bryant, but thankfully, Tommy shifts the direction of the conversation.

"Sam sent over the final numbers from the fundraiser, and it looks like everything you marked for luring a new vet should be covered."

"Good," I say, wracking my brain for any hints that Bryant might have given over the past few weeks to tell me if he's seeing someone. I'm coming up with absolutely nothing. "What else?"

"What else about your ex?" Tommy asks.

I roll my eyes. "I already explained that to you."

"So you say."

"I did!"

"Explain what?" Matt asks.

"Yeah, explain what?" echoes Chuck.

I give Tommy a withering look. "Sam and I weren't ever together. I told you this."

"No, you definitely did not."

Now it's time for Matt to get the same look.

"You didn't," he insists. "If anything, you complained about her dressing you up like a show pony, but that's it."

"Arm candy," I correct. "And we didn't date."

"Look at you getting all flustered," says Chuck as he grabs his second steak.

I let out a huff. "I'm not *flustered*. We went to functions together, yes. We weren't together though. She was super anxious about not knowing people and I—"

"You're you," Chuck interjects.

"Yes, I'm me. So we'd walk around together, I'd look like I was socializing and not on the market, and I'd introduce her to everyone, helping her meet people without the awkwardness of forgetting new names."

"That actually makes more sense than you two dating and you bringing her to the function you did."

I snort at Chuck. "It worked well enough for both of us."

"Maybe Bryant'll ask her out," he jokes.

I see Tommy's jaw twitch but don't say anything. Bryant groans as Chuck starts to hum "Here comes the bride" into his beer. Matt chuckles, likely imagining Bryant, tightly wound, surly, and buff, out on a date with Sam just chatting away.

"Anything else she has to say?" I ask Tommy.

"No, she just wanted to make sure everyone was on the same page for costs and exactly what gear was being purchased. We went over the various proposals and combinations and we should be all set by the end of the week for the first purchases to be made."

"Perfect."

Chuck tosses something across the table at Matt. "Where are you going tonight? The Rusty Spur or Maybel's?"

"Not sure, yet."

"Rusty Spur has a bachelorette party there tonight."

"And how do you know that?" Tommy asks.

Chuck shrugs. "A gentleman doesn't kiss and tell."

"You're not a gentleman," Matt says. "And you always kiss and tell."

"*I* don't tell," Chuck corrects, a cocky smirk spreading across his face. "But I don't stop the ladies from saying anything."

The rest of us groan.

Chapter 27
Avery

I park my mom's car near Jackson's house in Chet's usual spot since it's so close to the stables and he's done for the day. Jackson said he just needs to clean up before he can meet me there, so I head right over to the big open doors and breathe in the smell of horses, hay, and poop. A whole lot of poop. But I don't mind.

Living on a small farm and having acres of ranches nearby means the smells are just part of life. They let me know everything is working the way it should.

I hear someone near where the tack is organized, and I keep my boots quiet as I walk back there. Misty shakes her head and gives me a little neigh as I pat her soft nose to try to keep her quiet so she doesn't give me away.

After I get past her stall, I have a fantastic view of Jackson Landen's backside as he's pulling the saddle that I use from the stack. His muscles are straining under his shirt, and he is gorgeous.

Time for a little payback...

I'm rewarded with a "shit" as he spins around.

Actually, my real reward is being able to put my hand on Jackson's ass, which is exactly as glorious as I thought it would be. Even through a pair of jeans.

There's something in his eyes, and when he says, "Is there anyone else here?" I know it'll be a minute before I'm back outside.

And I'm more than okay with that.

I shake my head before he throws the saddle to the side.

In one stride he's erased the space between us and already has one hand tangled in my hair, tilting my head back, while the other is on my hip, tugging me closer. His eyes are hungry.

"Last chance to back out, Avery. I'm telling you right now, you don't have to worry about my feelings not being enough. Nothing about this is casual. But if you're concerned about anything and how fast or slow we should go, now's the time to say it."

With his forehead now on mine, he's making it almost impossible to think straight. I can see him struggling just the same. It's too early to tell him how I really feel, so I go for the obvious. "I thought I made myself pretty clear on the drive."

"You aren't having second thoughts or regrets?" His eyes search mine, the usually confident cowboy showing vulnerability just for me has my heart melting.

"My only regret is waiting this long to be with you, Jackson. Even if we need to keep things hidden for now."

His eyes close as he lets out a shuddering breath.

"For now."

"And we'll figure out how to tell Chase without losing him." I run my hands up and down his biceps, which is meant to comfort him but is only making me feel all sorts of things. "But first, we make sure we don't end up wanting to kill each other, yeah?"

"How long do we have?" The heat returns to his gaze.

I can't help the smile that spreads across my face knowing that look is only for me.

"At least an hour before the sun goes down and people expect me back. Why? Do you have somewhere better to be?" I ask, trying to tease him but realizing one of his brothers or ranch workers might be stopping by.

"The only place better would be in my bed," he says and dips his chin down so our lips meet in a slow, thorough kiss, like he's memorizing the sensation. I let my hands wander over his shoulders until they're behind his neck. I grab the back brim of his hat and toss it behind me, earning an appreciative sound from the back of his throat.

And then I feel his tongue flit out against my lower lip.

I'm not going to last long because I'm already trying to climb him like a tree to get my body flush with his as I open my mouth to give him all the access he needs.

Before I feel his tongue again, his hand releases my hair and travels down my back. And then, in tandem with the other, they scoop under my ass, lifting me up by my thighs.

It feels natural when my legs instinctually wrap around his waist and he straightens up, taking a few steps until my back is pressed against the wall. I can't wait any longer to taste his mouth and I let my tongue seek his.

God damn it. A man shouldn't be able to taste like this. He's minty, likely from brushing his teeth, but there's a salty flavor that has me squirming against him, wanting something to grind down on. But at this angle, for my head to be pretty much even with his, I'm afraid the bulge I so dearly want to rub against is too far south.

He breaks the kiss to look at me, a satisfied smirk on his face. "I can't tell you how long I've wanted this."

"Me, too," I say, feeling breathless.

"I've fucking dreamed about this so many times," he says as he buries his face in my neck, inhaling deeply.

"Just this?" My mind is already racing through the route to his place. He pauses before giving my neck a gentle nip with his teeth and raising his head so our eyes meet.

"No, baby. This," he rocks his hips and the motion continues up his spine, pressing us even closer, "and so much more."

I let out something between a groan and a moan. "Then show me everything."

Chapter 28
Jackson

Those four words unlock all of my restraint.

I crush my mouth against hers, reveling the feel of her tongue, now confident, against mine. If I didn't know these stables like the back of my hand, I would've had to break the kiss, but lucky for me, I can just secure her against me and turn around to grab a blanket.

With one hand, I pull it down from the wall, shake it out, and drop it on the floor. She hasn't stopped to ask what I'm doing and there's no way that I'm pausing, not when I have her wrapped around me like this. Kneeling down, I tip her backwards, bracing one arm so I can control how she's placed on the blanket. I pull back just enough to look down at her. She makes a sound of protest while tightening her legs around my waist and tugging harder around my neck to keep me planted.

Even though our hips aren't perfectly lined up right now, I still rock into her, and I'm as hard as if she were actually riding me.

If I hadn't felt them twice already, I wouldn't have thought lips this soft existed, but I find a way to create a little space. The look on her face, the impatience, is priceless.

"Calm down," I murmur against her mouth. "I just want to get closer."

Her hands immediately find their way to my chest, and she's already working the buttons. This time the noise she's making is one of urgency. Once she gets just enough buttons loose, I pull it over my head and am rewarded with her hands and mouth on my exposed skin before returning to my lips. I run my hand from her knee up her thighs.

God, she feels incredible and I give her a squeeze before I push the hem of her sundress up. She lies back, pressing down on her shoulders to lift her ass off the blanket so I can keep going. I want to look down so badly but I can't pull my mouth off hers when she's kissing me like she's been underwater for too long and I'm the first air she's had access to. It's like we're fucking each other's mouths because we refuse to separate. I've never wanted, no *needed*, to claim someone so thoroughly.

She pinches one of my nipples, causing my dick to jerk in my jeans and press painfully against the zipper. I nip her lower lip and pull back while tugging off her dress. She shifts so she comes with me and the dress goes right over her head.

I finally let myself look down.

I've seen her in bikinis, but this is different. Right now she's breathing hard with her lips swollen from what we've already done. She has a flush on her cheeks and those green eyes are scorching. Her wavy hair is spread out on the blanket like an auburn halo and she looks like an absolute goddess.

She starts to close the gap once more and I put a hand on her shoulder to keep her body from mine, just for a few moments, while my eyes travel down her neck to her shoulder. I reach behind her and with two quick pinches, I undo the clasp of her bra, letting it stay loose. My hand traces its way around her bra strap along the lacy edge where her breasts are just begging to be fully freed. I let my fingers, feather-light, trace a straight line from her cleavage down her soft belly. They circle around her bellybutton before dipping a little lower to follow the top edge of her underwear, which matches her bra. Both green, like the dress she wore the night of the auction.

I know this is early. I know. But I can't help but think that this is mine. That she's mine. That us being together isn't betraying the one person who has been there for me since we were old enough to talk. That I haven't been living the last ten years of my life going from unsatisfying relationships to momentary pleasures. That there's a chance I am actually going to get the one thing I've wanted.

She must sense a shift because she runs her hand up my arm until she rests her palm on my cheek. I instinctively lean into it. Her voice is quiet when she says, "What is it?"

And I give her the truth. "I gave up thinking that this might happen. Reality just sunk in that you're really here. With me. I locked that hope up so long ago." I shake my head, realizing she stopped moving while I explored her. "Sorry, I'm not usually like this."

She gives me a soft smile as she sits up. "Jackson, everything about this is real. I'm here. We'll figure this out. It might take time, but time is something we have. Now, I don't know what you're normally like with your romantic partners, and I don't really care. I just want you. The real you, however you are in each moment."

What the fuck have I done right in this world to have her here with me? I lean down to kiss her slowly and thoroughly before letting my body press her back down to the blanket. It's like we're melting together with her curves pressing against my chest, making her softness mold against me.

Chapter 29
Avery

Jesus. When I think I can't love this man any more, he goes and says something like *that*. Like he's wanted me and dreamed of me just like I've wanted him and dreamed of him over the years.

Everything with him is better than all of my fantasies so far, and that's saying something, as my vibrator can attest to.

I'm torn between ripping off the rest of our clothes to get him inside me immediately and just exploring. Kissing him is my new hobby, and I intend to become more than proficient at it.

The way his tongue commands its way into my mouth makes it hard to not squirm against him so I can rub my aching clit on something. But Lord have mercy, I don't know how much rational thinking I can do when any part of him is touching me. It's more than sparks, it's a goddamn fireworks show every single time.

His weight on me is delicious. I'm trapped in what might be my favorite place in the entire world. I let my hands run up his sides, feeling him shudder when they shift to the front and dip down by his belt. And then they make their way to his back in tandem, tracing over his defined muscles to his shoulders.

I need more.

I shimmy my arm to get my bra strap lower and it's like he senses what I'm doing so he languidly runs those calloused fingers up my arm to pull the strap down. He shifts his weight so his other hand can do the same without breaking our hungry kisses.

Lifting just his chest, he reaches his fingers between my breasts and with one firm tug, exposes them to the air. He trails kisses down my neck. I can feel his hand toss my bra away before it comes right back to cup my breast while swiping his thumb over my nipple, causing me to gasp. He flicks his tongue out against my collar bone and keeps moving down until his mouth is around my nipple and his tongue circles it.

"Yes," I say breathlessly, pressing up to give him all the access he could ever want. His finger and thumb start to mimic the motions of his tongue, making me moan.

He looks up at me, his eyes full of unbridled desire, nipple still in his mouth as his tongue gives it one last flick. I feel his hand trail down my side where he hooks a finger beneath my underwear.

"Do these need to stay on?" he asks, leaving my nipple for a moment, causing it to peak even more.

"Absolutely not."

"Thank God," he says, bringing his warm lips back to my breast. He tugs my underwear down, giving me enough space to lift my hips as his hand goes from one side to the other, bringing my final item of clothing closer to my ankles where I can slip fully out of them.

His hand travels back up my inner thigh and I'm not sure who makes the louder sound of pure pleasure when he runs his fingers through my folds. He's not even really doing anything at this point, just exploring, but I've been so turned on this evening, I know he feels it.

Jackson looks up, his eyes ablaze. "May I?"

"Only if you want to."

"Avery," he says, his voice becoming more serious, "I've wanted to do this exact thing for a very long time."

Well, that seals the deal for me and I push his head down, causing him to chuckle.

"Someone's in a hurry."

I squirm as his fingers keep exploring, but never enter me, to play with my clit. "You aren't the only one who's waited for this."

He trails kisses from my bellybutton as he shifts his bodyweight, causing me to shiver. Sometimes he nips at my skin and then licks it like he's soothing a wound. Each quick pinch followed by that tongue is maddening.

And then he freezes.

I look down and he's staring at my tattoo.

"Avery, what is this?" he asks, his voice deep and a little out of breath.

Oh boy, I was planning to give him a heads-up and forgot because he's so damn sexy in his cowboy hat and boots with his well-worn flannel shirt and jeans. Not to mention the belt.

"It's a tattoo," I say lamely, trying to remember what I was going to say earlier, but it's hard to focus with him settled between my thighs.

"I can see that," he replies while still staring at it. "What is it?"

Am I going to scare him off if I tell him the truth? Because it might make me sound obsessed.

"I got it a year ago, before I went back for classes."

He finally looks up at me and I expect to see an annoyed expression on his face, but he just looks like he's trying to temper his expectations.

"I know this horseshoe like the back of my hand, Avery. What's it doing on your body?"

If we're going to make it, we have to get used to being fully truthful.

"I got it a few days after your thirtieth birthday party, when I gave you the buckle," I begin, finally remembering my words. "I figured that we'd never even have the chance to do anything other than be friends because of Chase. I wanted something of you that I could keep as I tried to let go."

He looks down at the tattoo, which is the exact same horseshoe as the Landen Acres logo, just without the ranch name so it could easily be written off as a horseshoe for good luck. I can feel his warm breath as he gets closer to it, tracing it with his tongue, causing me to whimper.

Once he's satisfied with his physical inspection of the tattoo, his eyes are scorching when he says, "Don't ever be afraid to show me what's mine."

Chapter 30
Jackson

I'm an absolute goner.

When she approached me like that at the auction, I figured we'd need to take our time for her feelings to get anywhere close to mine. But this?

She fucking *branded herself* to have part of me when she thought there wasn't any hope. Shit, my rodeo ticket stub might not be something she laughs at.

Instead of continuing down her body, I lift myself up so I can kiss her again. I haven't fully told her how I feel, but I put it all in that kiss. Everything I've held back over the years, everything I've hidden, and everything I'll have to hide in public. For now.

Because she deserves everything and I won't settle for giving her anything less.

I break the kiss, causing her to open her eyes, and say a single word before heading back down her body: "Mine."

As she watches me kiss my way down her stomach, she whispers, "Yours."

I let out a groan deep in my throat as I push her legs further apart. I can see how ready she is for me and how much she wants this. My first lick starts at her core, moving up to her clit and my hands tighten as I lift her ass for better access. Her hands try to find purchase in my short hair as she presses my face into her even harder. If I wasn't so busy circling her clit, I would have smirked at her.

She twitches when my tongue directly crosses that bundle of nerves and I know she's climbing fast. Shifting my grip to free one hand, I work one and then two fingers into her, curling them to find that rough patch just inside of her. She whimpers and tries to grind down on my hand. I change my hold so she's firmly in place while continuing my ministrations.

"Oh my God, Jackson," she pants.

The combination of her taste on my tongue, my fingers deep inside of her, and her saying my name like that is driving me crazy and I pump harder while occasionally sucking on her clit to bring her closer.

And my view is exquisite.

Her breathing gets more ragged and her body tenses, lifting her shoulders off the blanket as she closes her eyes and her mouth falls open. The way her arms press her generous breasts together only adds to the experience as her fingertips press into my scalp.

I start to suck hard and flick her clit while holding the suction. She whimpers as her walls tighten around my fingers as she arches her back and her thighs press against the sides of my head.

And then she bucks, curling up in one big spasm as she cries out my name. I keep licking her while anchoring her hips in place as she moans and shudders through her orgasm.

My fingers feel each wave work its way through her body and everything gets wetter. Her breath hitches as she becomes over sensitized and she falls back against the blanket, bringing her hands up above her head.

I remove my fingers, locking my eyes on her as I lick the two that are now covered with her desire. She arches her back once more while closing her eyes and saying, "Oh my God, Jackson."

"So you've said," I reply before pressing a few wet kisses to her inner thigh and raising up so I can crawl up her body.

I rub my nose against hers, not sure if she's comfortable tasting herself, but then she plants one hand on the back of my neck and brings me in for a kiss that's all tongue with zero hesitation. I lower myself to her side and roll her so she's facing me. I run my hand down her side, tracing from the dip at the top of her hips all the way to her ass, which I happily rub.

"Can we take off your pants now, please?" she asks. "I need you inside me."

And here I thought she'd want to cuddle. Her kissing becomes more insistent as she releases her hold on my neck and trails her fingers around to my abs until she gets to the buckle.

"I don't think I have the ability to deny you a damn thing, Avery Barnett," I say honestly.

She unclasps the belt with one hand and uses both to undo the button and fly, finally giving my dick a little more room.

I hear a pouty sound come from the back of her throat. "Off."

I pull back to comply and she makes that sound again while tugging my face back to hers and pressing her breasts against my chest.

"Baby, you can't keep kissing me like this if you want me out of these pants."

"Make it quick, Jackson," she says before dipping her tongue into my mouth one last time.

I lean back so I'm sitting on my heels so I can get my boxer briefs down at the same time as my pants.

She's looking at my dick like she hadn't just put it in her mouth a few hours ago. I sit on my ass to remove my cowboy boots, tossing them in the aisle with my clothes.

Avery pulls me back over her and tugs me so my tip is brushing her curls.

"I'm on birth control and I'm clean," she says as she rolls her hips.

"I wouldn't have let you suck on me if I wasn't clean."

"Are you okay without a condom then?" she asks as one of her legs wraps around my lower back.

"Fuck yes," I reply right before she uses her foot to shove me inside of her, causing both of us to moan.

Chapter 31
Avery

Oh God, he feels incredible.

Jackson is in so deep that I can feel his balls laying against my ass and I just want *more*. He's completely filled me in a way I've never experienced before and the look on his face now that the shock of what I just did has worn off tells me I'm about to get exactly what I'm craving.

He leans down to nip my ear and murmurs, "Who said you were in charge?"

Then his tongue traces its way around the shell of my ear, making me shiver. He holds himself fully pressed into me and when I wiggle, one of his hands holds my hip still.

He makes a tsk, tsk sound and runs his teeth along my jaw before working his way to my mouth where his tongue mimics exactly what I want his dick to start doing. God damn, this man can kiss.

He keeps the pressure on my hip so I can't buck to get him moving and I've never been with someone who took control like this. He's driving me absolutely wild. I know I'm safe with him and that if I listen to his instincts, he's going to have me eating out of the palm of his hand in no time. Which is totally fine with me.

I match the rhythm his tongue has set and try to increase the intensity by pulling his face even closer to mine. His hand lifts a little but my hips remain perfectly still, which goes against everything my body is screaming for.

That same hand moves down my thigh and tugs so it's not wrapped around him and he presses my knee down and off to the side which gives him deeper access. I unwrap my other leg as I'm rewarded with him pulling out so just the tip remains inside of me, and in one full thrust, he buries himself right to the hilt.

I'm not ashamed of the sounds of pleasure that he devours with his lips.

I move one hand from his hair to his nipple, giving it a hard pinch, which makes his dick twitch deep inside of me. Jackson gently bites my lower lip and sucks it into his mouth, making me gasp and clench around him.

His eyes are on fire as he says, "You couldn't be more perfect, baby."

I've never had a guy call me "perfect" before. To hear someone like Jackson say it, someone who has known me my whole life, makes my heart ache with wanting him forever.

And then he starts up a steady pace where he pulls out enough so the ridge on his tip hits my G-spot with every single thrust, making that delicious pressure build deep in my core.

He's watching my face like he's cataloging how each adjustment he makes affects me and I can't take my eyes off his. The intensity tells me we're not just fucking, this is so much more. He's memorizing everything for our future and it's the sexiest thing I've ever witnessed.

I run my hand down his back, gripping tight and likely leaving marks. The thought of seeing scratches from my fingernails on his back in the days to come only turns me on more. If this didn't feel so damn amazing, I'd flip him over so I could ride him and leave a mark on his chest, too, but I don't dare change this angle or his rhythm as he's picking up speed.

Damn, when have I ever wanted to thoroughly claim a man in my life? I want the world, or at least the county, to see that we belong to each other and no one else.

I lift my hips to increase the pressure and he leans down for one deep kiss. When he pulls back, I grip the back of his neck to keep his face near as I say, "Mine."

His nostrils flare before replying, "Only yours."

He reaches his hand between us and starts to rub my clit, bringing me so close when he says, "Come with me, Avery."

I tense, unable to deny his command.

"Jackson." It sounds like a plea, but he keeps the pressure steady with his fingers while my breath comes in gasps.

"I've got you," he whispers, and I cry out.

Everything he built up explodes all at once. My legs wrap around him on instinct, and I ride out the waves of pleasure while he keeps slamming into me even though I can feel him coming as he grunts. I go limp as the bliss of the orgasm settles and he braces his arm next to my head. Our bodies are sweaty as I clench hard around him on purpose, causing him to make an addicting sound in the back of his throat.

I pull him tight against me, letting him collapse as we just breathe together, feeling our slick bodies slide a little. With my legs still around him, he seems to know that I'm not ready for him to pull out yet. I just need to hold onto this moment a little longer.

I know I'm not going anywhere and I trust that he isn't, either, but until we can figure everything out, this feels like a fragile haven where we get to play make-believe until reality sets in. My arms tighten around his neck and back, and I kiss his shoulder, tasting his salty sweat. He nuzzles the side of my head, making my hair even messier, but he doesn't seem to mind one bit as he breathes in deep.

Chapter 32
Jackson

We lie like this for a few more breaths before she unwraps her legs and I slip out. I already miss the feeling, so I roll onto my back and tuck her into my side so she can wrap an arm and a leg over me. This just feels natural. I tug on the blanket so we're partially covered. She releases a sigh, nuzzling her cheek against my chest and I run my fingers over her exposed skin.

"Tell me what's going on in that mind of yours," I say, placing a kiss to the top of her head.

"Just this," she replies, "and not wanting the moment to end."

"Soon enough, baby, soon enough and it won't," I say, holding her tight. "I promise."

I don't know what gives me the confidence to say those words and mean them, but I do. Wholeheartedly. Now that she's in my arms, we belong together, plain and simple. Maybe I should tone down my expectations to guard my heart. That's probably what a reasonable person would do. But I know, without a doubt, she's it for me. She's had my heart for years and I refuse to waste time questioning that.

As I bask in the feeling of having a completely naked Avery Jo Barnett curled around me, I can feel that things have shifted back to what all of this might mean. She's running her finger above my heart over and over. All I can think of right now is how amazing it's going to feel to have her draped across me in my bed.

This woman is everything I've dreamed of. She's stubborn as all hell, she makes me laugh, she somehow keeps me calm, she's absolutely stunning, she has the best smile, she's patient, she's kind, she loves Greenstone, and she's not afraid of farm and ranch life. She knows my history in this town, too, and she's still here, with a tattoo I'll need to inspect daily so I know it's real.

"What are your plans for this co-op?" I ask.

She smiles up at me. "You'll be invited to the first group meeting where you'll get all the details."

"That's it?" I ask, looking down at her face tucked against my chest.

"I have to organize everything and finalize the details now that I'm back." She props her chin up on the back of her hand so she can easily look at me. "Everything at school was related to Greenstone and the surrounding area but needed to be generalized for broader purposes. Now I get to tweak the data so it's truly tailored to our needs before I share anything."

"Doesn't being your secret-for-now boyfriend come with certain perks, like getting to hear about things early?"

She lifts her face and tugs mine down so she can kiss me. "Does this mean that Jackson Landen might have someone who he calls his girlfriend?"

I take my time kissing her thoroughly before answering, making sure she knows, without a doubt, what's on my mind.

"You're so much more than that," I say, pulling back enough so I can look at her. "*This* is so much more than that."

Chapter 33
Avery

His arms tighten around me and I hum in content. I catch myself before an "I love you" slips out of my mouth. I'm not putting any pressure on him, not after what he's been through. Plus, I don't want to scare him off. He handled seeing my tattoo just fine, but his reaction could have been more male pride than a declaration of love. I'm okay with giving him the time and space he needs to get there.

"When do you need to go for that ride?" he asks.

I look at him in confusion.

"Misty," he clarifies.

"Ah, yes, appearances. I suppose that means we can't stay just like this all night."

"No," he says. "But it does mean that you have to leave this and get dressed if you want to ride before dark."

"Good thing I packed riding pants for under my dress then."

"Let's see if you can get them on before the sun sets," he challenges.

"You just said that I should hop on a horse to make sure nothing is suspicious, I need to be clothed to do that, otherwise we'll raise too many questions."

"I wouldn't be asking you questions if you were out somewhere naked."

"Oh really?" I roll my eyes. "You'd have nothing to say?"

"I'm pretty sure it would be one of two situations."

"Which are?"

"Already being with me, which likely means we've gotten into exhibitionist activities. Or I scoop you up and take you somewhere that I can worship you without prying eyes."

"Those aren't the worst options in the world," I say. "But I don't think I'll be streaking any time soon, let alone having my way with you in public. Not that I haven't thought about it."

I kiss him before sitting up, not bothering to hold the blanket over myself. His eyes gleam as they take in my body. They pause at my tattoo and he traces over it with his thumb a few times before loosening his grip so I can stand up.

Jackson rolls to the side to grab my underwear and he sits up, motioning for me to come back. He holds them out for me to step into them, but when I reach down to pull them up myself, he tsks me as he takes over, kissing the skin ahead of where his hands are, like he's somehow tucking the kisses in by running the green lacy fabric over them.

I feel spoiled rotten by him.

He pulls my hip against his mouth as he takes his time showering it with attention. My hands are in his short hair and once more I'm amazed that this is happening.

"Tomorrow?" I ask, a little breathless again.

"Have lunch with Tommy at the big house and I'll steal you away. I'll even give you five minutes to hang out with him."

"Do you feel like you deserve a medal for your restraint?" I laugh.

"Absolutely," he says with mock seriousness, letting me step back. "I can't be sure that your tattoo is properly healed and it will need daily inspections."

"The tattoo I got a year ago?"

"You never know."

"You're right," I say, fastening my bra and pulling my riding pants out of my bag. He unfolds himself from the blanket, giving me an amazing view of his naked form while he gets dressed.

Once we're both clothed, with the exception of his shirt, he gives me another kiss and picks up the saddle that got tossed aside.

I sigh.

Soon enough, we won't have to sneak around and we need to use our time together wisely. No matter how much I want to toss him back down to the floor. I have to remind myself this is a marathon instead of a sprint. We have our lives to claw each other's clothes off.

Instead of putting Misty in front of the step for me, he ties her reins to the outside of the stall door and steps right in front of me with a smirk on his face.

"What are you—" I start.

He squats down, wrapping his big hands just below my ass, and scoops me up, causing me to yelp. This time, my legs are wrapped higher around him, closer to his still-bare chest, and he turns, hefting me so I'm sitting on Misty's saddle.

My hands are on his shoulders, and I'm still a little stunned at how easily he was able to toss me up here. His eyes are practically glowing with satisfaction.

I swallow. "Well, I guess that's one way to mount a horse."

"I'm not sure you're going to do it any other way from now on," he replies, squeezing my thighs before placing my hands on the pommel and backing away so I can toss my leg over.

I might demand this new method every day.

Chapter 34
Jackson

Watching Avery ride away on Misty just solidifies that this is where she belongs. Everything is so natural, and she doesn't hesitate to dive in.

I run my hand through my hair, remembering how her fingers felt in it just a little bit ago, and turn to go back into the stables. I currently have more horses here than usual since one of our stallions from the main stables is still recovering from a foot injury and was getting wound up not being able to run with the larger group. Grabbing the muck rake, I rub his nose and murmur a few words to him as I enter his stall. Checking all the corners, I fluff his still-clean hay, which isn't a surprise since I just mucked it out before I showered to calm my nerves.

I shake my head and wonder why I decided to look for horse shit right now. I pat his flank and look down at the tape job that I know is holding fast and leave the stall.

I throw a pair of work gloves on and eye up the last delivery of hay bales. My hands automatically reach out so my fingers can wrap under the baling twine, lifting the hundred-pound rectangles, walking them into the stables, and tossing them on top of one another until they're head-high before starting a new stack. Some people only get the lighter weight two-string bales, but our dad had us hauling three-strings ourselves by the time we were each fifteen and it always seems like a waste of energy to haul more bales to get the same end result.

By the time I hear hoofbeats approaching, I've worked up quite a sweat, but most of the bales have been taken care of.

Avery looks amazing. Half of what was in a ponytail now waves wild in the breeze and her cheeks are flushed. Misty couldn't look happier, either, as they slow to a walk, meeting me at the main doors. I look Misty in the eye. "Did she behave?"

Avery just laughs. "Of course I did. So did Misty; she's still my favorite horse." She leans forward to rub the horse's neck with a huge smile on her face.

I walk with them until we're at Misty's stall where she stops on her own. Avery swings one leg over so she's facing me and I offer my hand. She places her hand in mine but raises her eyebrow and clears her throat, tugging me closer.

Fully compliant, I step in front of her, pressing close to Misty so I'm between Avery's knees. She plants her hands on my shoulders and mine go to her waist. Instead of letting me lower her down though, she scoots off the saddle and wraps her arms and legs around me, planting a kiss right on my mouth.

I can smell Misty on her and the fresh evening air in her hair. One of my hands holds her ass and I wrap the other up her back and into what's left of that ponytail, holding her just right so I have all the access I could ever want to her mouth. She makes little sounds of pleasure in the back of her throat and I squeeze her ass, making her squirm in my arms trying to grind against me.

Misty releases a loud breath, bringing me back to reality. I loosen my grip and gently lower Avery, even though she makes a noise or two in protest.

"The sun's going down and your family will be expecting you," I remind her before she convinces me to have an actual roll in the hay.

"Is it okay that I already hate the 'secret' part of this?" she asks, adorably disgruntled.

"As if I don't?" I say, clenching my jaw so I don't suggest throwing caution to the wind and taking this public.

Instead of saying anything else, I follow my instincts and get on my knees in front of her, causing her to frown at me in confusion. Keeping my eyes on hers, I use one hand to lift her sundress and the other to tug at her riding pants. She whispers my name, thinking I'm about to do something different, not that I don't want to do *that*, but there's no time and that's not what this is about. When I see the ink, I dip my head down and kiss it, taking my time before she has to leave. Everything still feels surreal, but seeing this proves I wasn't the only one longing for us to be together over the years.

I put everything back into place as she moves her hands to my face and pulls me up to meet her mouth, claiming me as much as I just claimed her. Her tongue fights mine for dominance and I let her take complete control. Once she's satisfied, she breaks the kiss and I rest my forehead against hers and we stand like that for a few breaths.

I run my thumb over her cheek. "Tomorrow?" I ask.

"Tomorrow," she says.

I close the space for a more-chaste kiss. "I've got Misty, you head back home."

She nods.

"Goodnight, Jackson."

"Goodnight Avery."

I watch her walk towards my house, wanting nothing more than to be right beside her, heading in for the night.

Instead, I turn around and start taking care of Misty. Her ear twitches as I approach, and I run my hand along her back to let her know exactly where I am. Once I'm by her head, I start with her bridle, rubbing each spot where it pressed on her. As usual, she snorts when I walk around the corner to hang it up and nudges me with her nose when I return.

She's eager to go out with Avery, Chase, or me, but she's always impatient to get the saddle off afterwards. I secure the stirrups and unbuckle the girth before lifting it off her back. Avery's saddle feels light compared to mine and I wonder how Misty puts up with, let alone enjoys, hauling me around. Misty shows herself into her stall once I release her and open the door, just waiting to be brushed down. I double check that she has plenty of water before I check her for moisture or salt that I need to work off of her body.

I'm not surprised that I didn't find anything since she and Avery seemed to take it easy. I start rubbing circles on her with the curry comb. She's one of the few horses I've met who actually enjoys this process. When I first got her, she was apt to kick anyone touching anywhere near her back legs, but Chase kept her occupied with an obscene amount of sugar cubes that first day and now she lets me do anything I need to without a fuss. My heart squeezes and I grit my teeth. I know we aren't betraying Chase, but that doesn't mean keeping this trial a secret doesn't terrify me.

I can still hear that punch to this day. I've never seen Chase raise his hand to another soul any other time, but knowing his sister was hurt was too much for him to bear. I don't blame him. Hell, I was pissed, too. Susan and I always had less in common, she always dreamed of living off the farm and leaving Greenstone. But I've always seen her as a sister and could barely look at Jerry after that.

I can't let that happen to Chase and me.

Chapter 35
Avery

"How long do we have with you until Romeo whisks you away?" Courtney calls from her seat across from Tommy on the porch. The main house at Landen Acres has always felt inviting to me, even if it is absolutely enormous.

"What? No 'Hello, bestie,' or even a comment on the fact that I finally have my truck back?" I say with mock-hurt as I grab a tote from the bed of my truck before I go up the stairs to sit next to Tommy.

"I don't care what you drive and you know it," Courtney says. "I just want to know when to expect the man of your dreams."

I blush and grab a glass of iced tea to avoid responding.

"Don't think that we're not going to be talking about this just because he's my flesh and blood," Tommy says. "Just spare me some of the details."

"Don't you dare skip out on any details. I want them all," Courtney interjects before I can say a word.

"No thank you, that's my brother and I don't particularly want to hear about his skills in the boudoir. I've heard plenty over the years." He winces. "Sorry."

"I'm fully aware that he's had plenty of opportunities to practice. The whole town knows."

"And has all of that practice made him perfect?" Courtney asks.

Tommy sighs dramatically.

I fail to hide my smile or stop myself from blushing.

"He is! I knew it!"

"No. Details," Tommy says as he points his finger at me.

"Of course not. I don't let Ava tell me details, either," I assure him, grabbing a sandwich from the tray in the middle of the table.

"Fine, then give us details on what's going on because you've had to be vague," says Courtney.

"We're basically testing things out in secret. Well, as secret as we can get with you two knowing."

"And Chase?" Tommy asks.

My stomach churns a little thinking about the conversation we had just two days ago. Actually, it was less of a conversation and more of an argument, but that's a moot point now.

"Chase is why we're doing this trial. Ava and I have chatted a little, not about me and Jackson but just about her talking to Chase about backing off a little. In general."

"And you think that'll be enough?" Courtney asks with her mouth full.

"No, but we're not so naive to think that if someone hinted that we might be *together*-together, that he'd take it well."

"So how does this work then? How does he learn about you two seeing each other and not freak out?" she asks.

I take a bite of my sandwich before responding. "We didn't want him to know right away and assume that we would be a casual hook-up with Jackson ditching me. So, we're seeing each other, yes, behind Chase's back, to show him that it's not some fling."

Tommy puts his arm around me and kisses the top of my head. "We'll be your beard while you figure things out. But I'm going to be pissed if we don't start up a weekly game night soon."

"Deal."

We catch up on random things that have happened this week as we have our lunch together and it's not long before I hear someone coming down the driveway, causing butterflies to erupt in my belly.

"Look at her smiling and trying not to turn around to watch for him," Courtney teases.

"Wait, are your other brothers home?" I ask.

"Nope," Tommy replies. "Bryant and Matt are running errands, Chuck is checking the fence on the east end, and Jackson gave Chet the rest of the day off with full pay."

"Oh good." I realize things might have gotten awkward fast if one of them saw me hopping in and out of Jackson's SUV.

Tommy tips his head toward the vehicle that's coming around the bend. "Get down there so we don't have to watch him haul you off like a caveman."

I look from him to Courtney who just says, "Go," before winking at me.

"This is just temporary," I tell them, feeling guilty about cutting our time short.

"We know," Tommy says as he playfully shoves me out of my seat.

I turn and see Jackson nodding to Tommy and Courtney and giving me a glorious smile. I hop down the stairs and meet him right as he's turning in the circle they have in front of their house. He stops and I pull open the door, which just lets the oldies drift up to Tommy and Courtney who start singing along.

I hop into the passenger seat and before my door is closed, I feel his hand on the back of my head, bringing me in for a kiss. Like he couldn't wait one more second. The hand that just shut the door finds its way to his short hair to keep me anchored as he deepens the kiss and our tongues meet in a few strokes before he pulls back and nips my nose.

"Let's get out of here," he says, dropping his hand to my bare thigh.

"Yeah," I say, resting my hand on top of his as his thumb traces lazy circles. "Did you have time to eat?" I ask.

He looks over at me, already heading towards the highway. "It's a five minute drive to come and get you. That was plenty of time for me to have lunch."

"Fair enough. Tell me about the new horse."

"We just finished with everything, but I don't think he'll be here too long. He's a little easy to spook when there are other horses around so the original theory that his old injury came from another horse makes sense. So we got him settled in on the far side of the stables and I'll walk Misty down there a few times so he can get used to her from a distance at first." He squeezes my thigh. "What about your progress?"

"I started pulling more data about some of the biggest farms and ranches and adding it to the binders and the program I tweaked for my thesis."

"What does the program do?" he asks.

"It spits out projections based on historical values for units and prices and then uses current trends to predict three different possibilities given the variables you enter."

"And what did you tweak?" he asks.

"I changed the main market data from general cost-of-living and stock market values to also include the values of the main crops grown here as well as the livestock average worth each year."

"I always knew you were ridiculously smart," he says with a soft smile on his face.

"It was just telling it where to go to bring in more data."

"Maybe, but no one else thought to do that. Just you." He gives my thigh another squeeze.

He's right. I've always downplayed what I did with that program to get it to work for what I need so I could sell them on the practical uses of the data and how helpful it could be for modeling. But the trial and error of which data points to have it consider was a wildly time-consuming process. The end result though, has been incredibly useful in showing how small changes can help or hurt a family in the long run.

"Thank you," I tell him, picking his hand up from my thigh so I can kiss his knuckles, loving that we can simply be around each other.

Chapter 36
Jackson

Today is the true test of my patience and I'm already struggling as I hold her hand walking to my front door. We're greeted by Felix, our dad's old cat who meowed at the door for a few days when I temporarily moved back to the main house after our dad passed. When everything was settled and I was in my home again, Bryant showed up one morning with Felix in one hand and a bag of cat food in the other. He shoved them both at me before stomping back to his truck and bringing the rest of the supplies to my porch. He didn't say a word the whole time.

But Felix, he just purred and has been officially mine ever since.

"Hi buddy," Avery says, bending over to scratch the top of his head before he rubs against her legs.

I'm not surprised Felix already loves her. She hasn't seen him very much since he moved, but he used to cuddle with her when he was in the main house.

I put my keys on the holder inside the door where I hang up my hat and tuck my boots into place. Avery puts hers right next to mine and when she stands up, I put a knuckle under her chin so I can kiss her.

"We said—" she starts.

"I know, I know. That was just a welcome kiss. We have a no-sex rule for the next hour and I'm sticking to it." Somehow.

"Couch?" she asks.

I nod and grab two beers from the fridge before I sit next to her and hand her one. She shifts so her back is against the armrest and her bare legs drape across my lap.

"You're purposefully tempting me, aren't you?" I ask, tipping my head towards all the skin I have easy access to since she's got on another little sundress.

She rolls her eyes. "We never said cuddling was against the rules and we should face each other if we're talking."

"Uh-huh," I say, dropping my hand, which was recently holding her cold beer bottle, onto her lower thigh, causing her to jump.

"Evil."

"If I can't do everything on my mind, I might have to resort to riling you up in other ways."

She mock-glares at me. I just chuckle.

"I'll behave," I promise.

"Unlikely, but we'll go with that."

She clears her throat and lets out a little sigh before asking, "Did you know Chase converted his old bedroom into an office for me?"

She's quiet and I understand how she's feeling. Of course Chase did that without telling anyone. He shows he cares but he's always quiet about it. And it's like a punch to the gut knowing this has to be eating her up inside.

"And you feel guilty because of what we're doing?"

She nods.

"It's hard not to, even for me," I tell her. "But we should at least try to not look like a pair of impulsive and thoughtless assholes. If there's any room for doubt from him that this might not be more than a fling, then his nightmares will be true."

She nods as she picks at the label on her bottle. Over her dress, I massage her thigh.

"How about you tell me what he did to his old room? Did he take down his cowboy clock?"

"The clock is definitely still there in all its glory," she says, sounding lighter. "He got me a simple desk that has a dark stain finish and placed it under the windows with a flexible stand so I can work seated or standing. But the best part is the wall across from the closet."

"What did he do?" I ask.

"He blew up a county map so it fills half of the wall and he color-coded and outlined every ranch and farm with a key that gives a summary of the property and then corresponds to a binder of the same color. Each binder has a page in a protective sleeve with the family's information, sales history, crop or herd data, and contact information. I might have tested it out a little when I saw it."

Pulling her close, I hug her and kiss the top of her hair, breathing in that peach scent. "Of course you did. That was one hell of a graduation gift."

"I know he's proud of me for being the first person in our family to get an advanced degree, and I know he knows what I studied, but I didn't realize how much he really listened to what I was hoping to do."

"I feel like I should be surprised, but I'm not. That fits Chase to a T."

She chuckles. "Pretending to be slightly oblivious and then quietly doing something huge to show he's proud?"

"Showing he cares in his own way," I reply. I pause a moment. "Do you know what he did for me after my dad died?"

She shakes her head, reaching a hand out and interlocking our fingers.

"A few weeks after the funeral, I had an appointment with the lawyer to go over what was needed to run the ranch. Bryant wanted to come, but since I was the one inheriting and Matt was *almost* eighteen, I wanted to make sure no one else had to panic if there was even a small possibility he would need to live with our mom."

I take a breath, remembering that day. It was the last time I yelled at Bryant, really yelled at him. I know he meant well, wanting to come, but I was barely holding it together as it was and needed to keep my head on straight for the meeting. I squeeze my eyes shut tight for a moment. I've never told a soul about how terrified I was that we would have to send Matt across the damn country for the rest of his senior year. All to live with the woman who hated this place.

Chapter 37
Avery

"Chase knew that I was struggling with being the one everything fell to. And that morning, I went to saddle up Misty to clear my head and in front of her stall was a binder." He clears his throat. "He had laid out possible custody options showing that I had to claim Matt as my legal ward and explained it in ways that my jumbled brain could understand. For the first time since the accident, I felt like I wasn't suffocating. I've always known that it would be my name listed first on the deed when the ranch was handed down, so I was prepared for everything that goes into Landen Acres. But not Matt.

"That was the last day I cried. I knew I had a strong enough case, along with..." He pauses once more. I release his hand for a moment so I can wipe a tear that has fallen down his cheek. He clears his throat. "Along with thirty-three certified statements from community members providing testimony that, not only could I be Matt's legal guardian, but that the home the five of us had was stable, loving, and the best thing for him. All because of Chase."

My heart breaks for him and how alone and helpless he felt. "I remember him leaving for hours each day for interviews. He had us all believing they were to make sure that the ranch went to you. Not about Matt," I say, gently turning his face to look at me. "I'm sorry that you had to go through all of that pain on top of losing your father."

He meets me for a kiss, this one tender and slow. Our foreheads press together as we simply sit here. I don't know that I've ever felt this comfortable or this at-home as I do right now. I want to kiss away every tear and erase the pain he went through thinking he might lose Matt while grieving his father with no one to guide him.

I only have vague memories of their mom. She was around a little, but I don't remember her ever socializing or even talking with other people the way my parents did. And then one day, she left. Chase later said that when she asked for a divorce, Jackson's dad only had one request: to keep the kids on the ranch if they wanted to stay. She moved back to the coast where she felt at home and only visited a few times. Chase said he overheard our parents talking one night where they mentioned she felt trapped here in Greenstone. That she craved life in a big city. That she tried to make it work, but she needed something different, something somewhere else.

"All of that is in the past," he says. "I just want what's here now."

"I feel the same way," I reply.

He takes a swig from his bottle and takes a breath. "Okay, how do we move this to the next step?"

"Says the guy who hates dating."

"Says the guy who couldn't date the one person he actually wanted."

And that has me shivering with delight. A smile slowly grows across my face and his hand squeezes my thigh.

"I think we need to find a way to spend more than an hour together each day because we already know what we usually spend that time doing."

"So are you proposing a weekend away? That might be a little obvious to everyone if we're suddenly both gone."

"Agreed, that's way too obvious," I say. "We could do an overnight, but not away."

"I get to have you for a full night?" he asks.

"Yep. I'll sneak out, just like a teenager. You pick me up and get me back well before five the next morning."

"When?"

"Sunday night?"

"Done," he says without needing a moment to think it over. "Just tell me when to be there."

Chapter 38
Jackson

"I'm the only one who stays up much past eight on the entire property, except Ava and sometimes Chase, so I can easily meet you at nine."

"I'll be there at eight-thirty." I wink at her. I've never been this open about wanting to see someone. Granted, I've never felt this strongly about anyone, but it's freeing.

She leans in, placing one hand on my cheek, and kisses me. "I'll be there at eight-thirty then."

Before she can pull away, I nip her bottom lip and kiss it, unable to resist.

"Alright, let's talk about the big things and get them all out in the open so we know what we have different opinions on or expectations about," I propose before I ignore our rule for this date.

"Okay," she agrees. "I want kids, but I don't need them soon and I don't need a lot of them. How's that for a start?"

"I figured we'd start smaller, like with if or how we see our jobs changing, but let's cover kids," I say, taking another swig of my beer. "For the last, heck, almost ten years, I really didn't think I'd have someone to raise a family with, but part of me always assumed I'd be a dad. Becoming Matt's legal guardian didn't really change how I saw him. So, while one might say I have been, and therefore still am, a dad or at least a father figure, he was always my kid brother. I just had to sign forms for a while before he was legally able to."

She reaches out and grabs my hand, entwining our fingers.

"Apparently, I become a chatterbox around you when it comes to things I don't regularly talk about," I admit. "But I'd say that we're pretty much on the same page for kids. I just know that it'll be a little while before I'm ready to share you with anyone."

"Okay," she says. "Then let's talk about our jobs. If this co-op really starts to function well, then I'll have a handful of meetings to go to throughout the year, likely in the evenings, but otherwise, everything else can be handled remotely."

I barely hesitate to ask, "Where do you see your home?"

"It depends."

"On what?"

"If my boyfriend wants me to move in or if he'd like to get a different place."

It might take some effort to not kiss her senseless when she refers to me as her boyfriend, even if I'm thirty-one.

"Do you have a preference?"

"I do, but I'd like to hear yours since you own your home."

"I built it, I didn't buy it," I say.

"True," she says. "But you know what I mean."

"Yeah, I do." I smirk at her. "And I have a preference. This ranch is technically in my name, but it's also in my blood. I'd like to live here if you feel like it wouldn't be a sacrifice. But if you need something different, I'll do it."

"Really?" She looks surprised.

"Within reason. You know I'd be lost in the city," I say.

"It's a good thing this ranch always felt like home to me then, isn't it?"

I swallow, not wanting to speak too soon.

"What? You have nothing to say?"

I shrug. "I was making sure you weren't going to immediately take those words back. Plus, you haven't actually said what your preference is."

She looks around the room with a content expression. "Here."

Nothing could hold back my smile in this moment. "Here it is, then."

I clear my throat, remembering something I meant to bring up earlier. "To be fully transparent, I want you to know only a few people ever came back here with me. And much to the disappointment of some, it was never anyone I had more than a one-night thing with."

"Good to know," she says with a little note of apprehension.

"And as for Sam," I say, getting her full attention, "she and I weren't really together."

She looks skeptical. "She approached me at one of her first socials. Tommy was sick and I filled in for him bringing drinks. She was clearly trying to cover up her nerves and I asked her if she wanted to be introduced to anyone since she was new. She looked relieved and we struck a bargain since I was supposed to be present at two more events that month. We'd show up together, I'd introduce her, she'd do the rest of the talking, and I'd look like I wasn't hating every moment of being there. Apparently, I have a hard time hiding my resting bitch face."

Avery snorts a laugh. "So were you ever...you know?"

"We kissed once and figured out there was nothing there and that's it. We let everyone think we were together for a while and it kept a few people off my back who wanted, well, you know what they wanted, and she got to meet people without feeling awkward. Which means you don't have to hate her."

She lets out a breath. "Was it obvious?"

"Just to me. But I think you two would actually get along and you could work together to help the county and your co-op. Have Tommy set something up."

"Why Tommy? Why not you if you weren't together?"

"Because she gave me a nickname." I wince.

"She did not!" Avery sits up straight and smacks my arm. "What is it?"

"I shouldn't have said anything."

"Tell me or my request for my home will be the big city," she threatens.

"You wouldn't."

"No, but I want to know," she laughs.

"Fine," I mumble, knowing I'll never be able to deny her anything. "Jacksy."

Chapter 39
Avery

I burst out laughing, I can't help it. I would have spit my beer all over him if the timing had been right. Just looking at his face right now says it all.

"She said it in public, within earshot of someone I was trying to avoid, and I thought she was either kidding or laying it on thick in front of them." He runs a hand down his face.

"I'm sorry that your fake girlfriend gave you such an epic nickname," I say, rubbing his arm and trying to contain my giggles. "How did I not hear about this?"

"It wasn't *that* public, but your brother definitely knows about it."

"Poor, Jackson."

I do feel better hearing about their arrangement. I know he's "seen" people for a while and actually dated someone in college, but I'll admit that things seemed different, at least according to general small-town gossip.

"Okay, we've covered kids, housing, and exes. What about a workspace?" I ask, taking pity on him.

"I have an office upstairs," he says, like it explains everything.

"I've only ever been on the main floor and I don't think we were able to fit in a tour of the house yesterday since we didn't leave the stables."

"I know I was a little preoccupied. Let's go up and I'll show you around." He leans in for a quick, but intense kiss, causing my lips to chase his for just a little more before we part.

I shift so my feet are on the floor and we get up, his arm going around my waist, like it's hard for him to not make contact. He's not the only one.

We head past the couch and through the dining area. Nothing on this level is closed off, besides the bathroom, so I wouldn't call it a dining room, but it's definitely note-worthy. The table itself reminds me of the rest of the house with the natural wood being the focus. The table is big enough for at least eight people, which isn't a surprise since the brothers are so close. I can imagine everyone gathering here, even Chase, and there's a bittersweet feeling in my chest for a moment.

He guides me so I'm first going up the stairs, which are fairly wide. When we reach the top, he tips his head to the right and I walk through the open doorway of the first room to find a sunny space.

"Oh wow, it's bigger than I expected," I say, turning towards him.

"I've heard that before." He winks at me with a knowing smirk and leans against the doorway with his hands in his pockets. I roll my eyes before turning back to the room.

There's a wall of bookshelves and everything is organized and neatly spaced. He has a record player on a little stand in the corner with two shelves of records, all oldies based on the titles I can see. There's a desk that's open underneath and a gamer chair pushed in before a few monitors and a tower with an ergonomic keyboard. The monitors are angled so he can look out the window and see the stables.

There's one free-standing filing cabinet, but otherwise, the office is bare without feeling cold. Everything has its place and the tidiness is endearing.

"So," he says, walking up behind me and wrapping his arms around me. "Will we be able to fit all of your things in here, or do I need to knock out a wall?"

I tip my head back so I can look at him. "You really want to share an office? What if I'm an absolute slob?"

"I know how messy you can be, but I'd be crazy not to share everything with you."

"Yeah, we'll see how long it takes until you change your mind," I say, partially teasing because I'm not a slob, but I'm not as neat as he is.

He holds my chin so I can't look down. "Not. Happening."

The look in his eyes just reinforces his determination, making my heart beat so hard I'm sure he can hear it.

"No take backs?" I ask.

"None."

"Okay then, this will be *our* office."

He leans down just as I reach a hand up to grab the back of his neck. This kiss feels like we're sealing our future together. His mouth moves perfectly over mine and he holds me in place with one arm while his other hand slowly moves down my throat. Neither of us pull back from the kiss as we explore each other's mouths as if we haven't been doing this every chance we get. I feel his hand continue its path downwards until it's brushing the top of my sundress, which happens to have an elastic bust, offering him easy access to slip in and run his fingers over my nipple. He consumes the sounds I make with his mouth before he pulls his hand out and groans.

"Sorry, I momentarily forgot our one rule for today," he says, his voice husky as he kisses my jaw before he whispers with his nose nuzzling my hair. "I'll make it up to you when you stay over, I promise."

I shudder with anticipation, relishing the feel of him pressed against me with his breath in my ear. All I can do is nod while he nips my earlobe and try to remind myself why we have a no sex rule.

He stands up, keeping his arm around me, clears his throat, and turns us so we're facing the wall opposite his desk. "I was thinking the map could go here."

Could he be more thoughtful? I take a deep breath to ground myself in the moment and lace our fingers together. "I would love that," I say.

Jackson goes still for a moment and then steps back, confusing me. I start to turn to see where he's going but he circles around me so we're facing each other. His jaw is clenched and there's a look of intensity that I don't know I've seen before on his face. I can't figure out what has him so stressed all of a sudden.

"Hey," I say. "What's wrong?"

He shakes his head before saying, "Nothing. Nothing's wrong."

I rub his arm with my free hand because I'm worried by the emotion in his eyes. "What is it, Jackson?"

Both of his hands find their way to my face so he's cradling it as he steps forward and never breaks eye-contact.

"Avery Jo Barnett, I'm in love with you."

Chapter 40
Jackson

Hearing her say the word "love" made something in me snap, even if she wasn't saying she loves *me*.

I think I should be panicking right now, but I feel steady, calm. This is the one thing that I've been sure of for years and while she might need time to say anything back, I know she's just as committed to this as I am.

Her big green eyes are locked with mine as I ramble on. "And I think I've made it clear that I've felt this way for a long time. I know that we've only been testing things out for a few days, really, but I know this is it for me. You're everything I've been dreaming of. We still have things to figure out and sneaking around behind Chase's back is one of the shittiest things I've ever done, but knowing that you're with me? That makes it worth it. I don't mean to scare you off," I use my thumb to wipe a tear that fell from her cheek, "but this office, it's ours. It stopped being mine the moment we kissed. It's okay if you're not where I'm at. It's okay, baby. But I just needed to tell you that everything that's mine is ours. You've held my heart long enough without me saying something and I'm done keeping it inside."

I lean down so I stop my babbling with a final "I love you," and kiss the woman of my dreams. The woman who's in my arms.

The kiss is slow with her tongue finding mine every time. I can feel another tear hit my hand and I pull back, making sure she's okay. Her hands grab the back of my neck to keep me from creating too much space.

"Jackson, I've been wanting to say the same thing to you, I just didn't want you to feel pressured." Her eyes are wide with emotion. "I love you. Only you."

I crush my mouth against hers as I scoop her up by the back of her thighs. She feels like home. Her legs around me feel like home. Her mouth on mine, her hands in my hair, her chest pressing into mine? Home.

I walk over to the edge of the desk, ridiculously grateful that I'm a bit of a neat freak because taking a hand off her curves to sweep shit out of the way would be too big of an ask. I lay her down and her legs stay in place, holding our bodies flush. Our kisses deepen as she relaxes against the wood, and I can't get enough.

I hold myself back from inching up her dress because today is about really figuring out how we fit, how we argue, what we need stocked in the pantry, and those things. But I'm only human, so I allow my hand to trail over her dress from her hips, dipping at her waist and cupping her breast. She makes a needy sound, so I play with her nipple, which I can tell is hard even through the fabric of her dress and whatever bra she has on today.

Avery whimpers and I devour it while pressing down against her hips as she tries to grind against my abs. God, she feels incredible. I'm already addicted to each little sound she makes, the way her hair smells like peaches, how her curves allow me to grab on and hold her tight. I feel every inch where our bodies press together and I don't know that this pulsing desire for her can ever lessen.

I'm fighting my instincts to get closer, to feel her writhe under me as I make her come, but I keep our clothes firmly in place and put everything into these kisses. Her hands explore my shoulders and back as she rocks her hips into me again. I pull my mouth off of hers and kiss my way to her ear that she immediately gives me access to. Brushing her hair away, I gently scrape my teeth along the lobe and press feather-light kisses just behind it. I feel her breasts press against me, filling the hand that's cupping her right one. She fits me perfectly and I'm going to be throwing her on my bed if I don't pump the breaks.

I nuzzle behind her ear and slowly kiss my way back to her lips, moving my hand from her breast up to her chin to have her turn her face exactly where I want it. Our tongues meet once more with a final sweep before I feel her relaxing as our foreheads meet. I close my eyes and just breathe this moment in, listening as her panting slows, feeling her hands gently run over my back until they rest on my sides.

"If I promise to be good, can I make sure everything is healing properly?" I ask.

She lets out a soft giggle. "The year-old tattoo?"

"That's the one."

She nods at me and instead of kissing my way down, because I wouldn't be able to stop, I trace one hand from behind her ear over her throat and trail it over her dress, lifting myself off her enough so I can see my progress. When I reach her hip, the hem of her dress is easy to push out of the way. I tsk.

"You were supposed to behave today," I tell her, running my finger along the top edge of her lacy, purple, flimsy excuse for underwear.

"It's not my fault you're looking," she says.

I follow the pattern until I'm on the side of her hip and hook my finger through, tugging down just enough to show the entire horseshoe.

"Hold this," I murmur, and her hand drops to keep the lace in place as I trace the shape, barely touching it. I feel her goosebumps before I see them and I resist the urge to kiss the tattoo, to draw more from her skin. Instead, once I'm satisfied that it's real, that she's real and in my arms, my fingers find their way to hers, letting the lace fall back into place. I lean over her again, brushing a stray hair from her face.

"Let me show you the rest of our house before we run out of time today." I don't even hesitate to call the house anything but ours.

She rubs her nose against mine. "I like the sound of that."

I stand up, wrapping my arms around her back to bring her with me as she unhooks her feet and lowers them to the floor. We automatically hold hands as I lead her out of the office.

"This is an extra bedroom," I say, opening the next door so she can peek inside. There's not much to see because it's empty, so we go to the next door that's already open.

"Bathroom," I tell her, releasing her hand as she walks in. It's a standard tub/shower combo, a toilet, and a double-sink vanity. Everything is simple and I wonder if it's too different from what she's used to after living in the city. She has a soft smile on her face as she grabs my hand and leads us across the hall.

"And this one?"

"Another bedroom," I say, resisting the urge to justify the double bed. I set it up in case one of my brothers needs to cool off for a night and not for any of my exes.

"There's only one more door," she notes, facing me with a knowing look in her eyes, and I just nod.

Dear God, if I follow her into my room, we're not leaving for hours.

Chapter 41
Avery

Jackson has been oddly quiet during this tour and I'm not sure why, so I don't comment on what I see.

He built a home for a family.

Hell, the bathroom has two sinks, which makes me picture multiple kids sharing it. Just like the main level of the house, things are tidy, simple, and beautiful in their own way.

We make our way down the rest of the hallway, which definitely needs something on the walls since they're totally bare. I imagine putting up a photo of all five brothers with their dad. Jackson doesn't really have many pictures anywhere in the house, I'm not sure he's thought about putting them up, but I think he would like it after all this time.

He opens the door that was barely ajar and I stare. I didn't expect his bedroom to look like this. It's by far the biggest room upstairs and his huge windows light up the space even though the sun isn't shining directly in.

I take a step in as he releases my hand so I can wander. He has a king-size bed along one wall and in the far corner, what appears to be a jacuzzi. There's a glass wall that distorts things, but I can see a half-bath on the other side, but no door. I turn back and look at Jackson with a raised eyebrow.

"I don't need privacy from myself," he says as he shrugs. "I don't bring anyone up here, but we can add a door and frost the glass."

He mentioned before that he really didn't bring people back to his place, but I assumed that *someone* had been in his room overnight.

I nod at the tub. "I didn't take you for a spa kind of guy."

"The main house has three of these upstairs. We take our sore muscles very seriously," he says in mock-solemnity. He's still in the doorway, leaning against the frame like he was in the office. Like he's just letting me explore while watching my reactions.

There's one long dresser, a full-length mirror, and a huge-looking closet. I walk up to the door and watch Jackson as I slide it open, making sure I'm not crossing any boundaries. I don't expect he planned on letting me inspect his house today like this. He gives me a little nod.

I stifle a giggle.

Jackson Landen, the man who wears well-worn flannel shirts and jeans that he put holes in from working in them so much, hangs up *all* of his clothes. On the far end of the closet, I can see his suit that he wore to Chase's wedding in a clear, zipped bag, but then he has a pants hanger that's open on one end filled with his work jeans. I look back at his shirts and even the ones he cut the sleeves off are on hangers.

"Why?" I ask, gesturing to the closet. He looks like he was expecting my question.

"I hate, and I mean *hate*, folding clothes, especially shirts with buttons."

"Oh my God, you're adorable. You hang up your work clothes so you don't have to fold them."

I close the closet and walk over to him. "What happens if someone else folds your clothes, are you okay with that? Or is it just that you like things hung up?" I ask, wrapping my arms around his waist and loving the feel of him holding me without hesitation.

"I have no issue with my clothes being folded. I just hate folding them myself."

"Such a reasonable solution you found," I tease, imagining him grumbling over his attempts at folding and then shoving his clothes on hangers.

"Is there a reason you haven't entered any of the rooms with me besides the office?" I ask.

"There wasn't much to see in the other rooms, and if I cross this threshold, you're not leaving this one for several hours."

Heat pools low in my abdomen as he presses me flush against him, snakes one hand out to tip up my chin, and kisses me slowly. My eyes flutter closed as I let him take over, feeling his chiseled abs against my chest and his hardening erection against my stomach. His hand moves to my hair and he groans, breaking the connection. He kisses my forehead to cool us both down before I drag him to his enormous bed.

"I'm really the first person to be in your room?" I ask.

He nods. "Besides my family members and Chase, when it was being built."

"Well, we'll just need to break things in soon, won't we?"

Heat flares in his eye. "Absolutely."

So much for cooling us both down.

I take the lead and tip my head towards the stairs to remove the king-sized temptation behind me. "Kitchen?"

"You've seen the kitchen," he replies.

"Not in an I-might-cook-here-one-day sort of way."

He halts us right before the first step down, crowding my personal space. He all but growls a single word.

"Might?"

I smirk at his almost-possessiveness. We both know I love to cook and bake cookies.

"Will," I concede. Not that it was a hardship.

He nods and takes the lead, apparently satisfied with my correction, which makes me smile. Something broke free in Jackson since we made this secretly official and his openness continues to give me butterflies in the best way possible.

When he steps off the landing, I hold still and tug on his hand, turning him around. We're closer to the same height than usual and I don't have to pull his face more than a foot to kiss him from here, so as I put pressure on the back of his neck I say, "I love you," and kiss him softly, just because I can.

He pulls back and gives me one of his unguarded smiles that lights up his whole face and says those three words back to me. "Should we go decide where your cookie-baking supplies are going to live? Because I might request a full batch of your oatmeal chocolate chunk ones at least once a week."

As we make our way to his kitchen, which is simple, but fairly spacious, my breath catches for just a second. *This* is going to be our lives. I can see it, I can feel it, and I can taste it.

Chapter 42
Jackson

Everything feels different now, more real. Watching Avery claim the pantry shelves that she wants specifically for baking supplies makes me feel like I just won the damn lottery. I stand behind her and wrap my arms around her and she answers my questions about how things should be organized in here, and even in the dishwasher because, according to her, I load my plates backwards.

And here I thought I was going to be the more particular one.

We sit and talk in the oversized armchair next to the couch, she's fully curled up in my lap with her hand on my chest and her head resting on my shoulder. I run my fingers up and down her calves while my other hand is tucked against her stomach. We disagree about getting a dog for this part of the ranch, we have three at the main house, and she wants to not stress out Felix in his old age. I guess it's good that I haven't followed through on getting one because that can wait.

Our time ticks away and she unfolds herself from my lap with a resigned sigh before we head to the door.

I glance down at our boots sitting side-by-side and it makes me wonder...

"How soon can we tell him?" I ask.

Avery looks up at me with those beautiful green eyes. "Not today?" She laughs. "I can't imagine he'd take it well if we waltzed right up to him and told him we have it all figured out within a few days of me moving back."

"Don't we?" I ask, completely serious.

I hear her take a sharp breath in. "*We* might have most things figured out, Jackson, but even Tommy would look at us funny if we told him that."

I take a deep breath. "Okay, so let's talk about timelines."

"Alright, anything more than a month will likely just hurt him more."

"Not to mention that I'm not going to last a month with only seeing you in secret." I don't even mention that my other brothers will likely catch on quickly with me stealing her away from the main house. Our boots are on and I hold the door open and put my hat on while she scratches Felix under his chin as he's sunning himself near the entryway.

She leaves the house ahead of me and turns to face me when I mumble, "One sec."

While I know Bryant and Matt won't be back until dinner tonight, I don't want to risk Chuck being back at the main house early, so I pick her up in my favorite way, bringing her legs right around my waist. She lets out a little squeak of surprise but snatches my hat in her hand as she closes the space between our mouths. I don't press her back against anything, I just stand on my front porch holding Avery with one hand cradling her ass and the other already tangled in her hair, keeping her right where I want her.

She nips at my lower lip and I follow her little retreat, covering her mouth with mine, feeling them move in sync. A sound escapes my throat as she somehow presses her entire body into mine and my dick is hard once more. This woman turns me on like no one else.

Before I do something that will definitely make us very late, I give her a slow kiss and feel her fingers run up and down the back of my neck. I open my eyes to see her staring right back at me and she gives me a smile.

"I love you, Jackson."

"I love you, too, Avery."

With her legs still wrapped around me, I pull her close, tucking her cheek against mine. Her arms overlap behind my neck and we stay like this for a moment, just holding each other.

"You ready to go back to pretending a little longer?" I ask.

"Not really," she says with a sigh.

"Same."

She pulls back and gives me one more kiss before we detangle ourselves and she's back on her own two feet. We walk down the porch steps and I open the passenger door for her when both of our phones vibrate.

Tommy: Chuck is home and just went upstairs to clean up, you have about 10 minutes. He thinks Avery is just in the bathroom on the main floor.

"Good thing it's only a five minute drive, right?"

"Right," I reply, crossing in front of my SUV to hop in the driver's seat and get going.

Avery's hand reaches for mine right after I put it in drive, her thumb tracing little circles against the back of my hand.

"Did you call Rebecca?" she asks.

I frown, trying to place the name.

"The vet," she says. "You're supposed to woo her into finding a place here in Greenstone."

"Shit, I meant to set a reminder before walking to Chase's house after moving you in." I grab my phone from its stand, unlock it, and hand it over to Avery before turning off my driveway and onto the gravel road connecting the houses. "Want to send her something now to set up a meeting or call?"

"You want me to write it out?"

I shrug. "Why not? Just don't make it sound too formal."

"Okay." Her head is down as she types out the message and I hear the "send" sound. "Done."

I look over at her.

"What?"

"You didn't invite her to our overnight, did you?"

She laughs. "Absolutely not. I have no intention of sharing our alone time with anyone."

Putting my phone back, I grab her hand and bring it to my mouth so I can kiss her knuckles. "Me neither."

We're turning onto the long gravel driveway to get to the main house much sooner than we'd like. I park next to the house instead of in my usual spot so Chuck doesn't see Avery hopping out of my SUV from upstairs. She gives me a questioning look.

"There's some paperwork that I need to grab from inside," I explain as we walk up the steps to the porch where Tommy and Courtney are lounging. Courtney gives us a knowing look and Tommy throws a chip at her.

"He's still upstairs," Tommy tells us, keeping his voice low. "The water was still running when I got a refill less than a minute ago."

Avery lets out a breath of relief and, because I can, I grab her ass as I walk to the door, looking back to see her face turn beet red.

"Just practicing," I say, giving her a wink and ignoring Tommy and Courtney's laughter.

Chapter 43
Avery

I watch Jackson walk into the house. My face is burning, but I can't hide my smile.

"Sit down for the three minutes we have left before we head back to our so-called jobs," Tommy says, waving me over to my old spot.

Courtney raises an eyebrow and looks me up and down.

"We didn't do *that*."

"Courtney," Tommy warns. "No. Details."

"There are none to give, Tommy. You're fully in the clear."

Courtney lets out what could be categorized as a "harrumph" before mumbling, "Well, you two are no fun."

"The point of today was to give us time to be together without *being together*. To test the whole relationship piece out versus the physical."

I hear Tommy groan dramatically at that last word.

"So, what happened?"

The blush that was going away comes back in full force. "We might have said a few important words out loud..."

Courtney looks confused and Tommy swats my arm.

"He said it?" he asks, wide-eyed.

I nod.

"What? What am I missing?" Courtney asks.

Tommy just holds up his hand, raising only his thumb, pointer-finger, and pinky.

"Oh my God! How did it happen? Tell us *all* the details!" Courtney squeals.

"Shh," Tommy warns, tipping his head toward the house. "Chuck."

"We were checking out the office—"

"That better not be a euphemism."

"No interrupting," I tell Tommy. "And it was a tour since I never had a reason to go upstairs before. We were in the office and it happened when we were talking about where my big map from Chase would go."

"Who said it first?" Courtney whispers.

I look at the door and nod my head in the direction Jackson went. She squeals, runs around the table, and throws her arms around me from one side as Tommy does the same from the other.

"You said it back, right?" Tommy asks.

"Yeah, I definitely did."

We hear footsteps inside the house heading our way and we start gathering up the plates and glasses from the table, almost like we're teenagers trying too hard to look casual.

Jackson comes out the door, looking at his phone. "You around Sunday afternoon?" he asks Tommy.

"Yeah."

"Okay, there's a vet who's stopping by to talk about the opening and the fundraiser. Can you get the final numbers from Sam along with Dr. Harris's stats from his last active year?"

Courtney and I walk into the kitchen to put the plates and my glass in the dishwasher, everything is so quiet that I can't *not* overhear their conversation.

"Yeah, I already pulled that info, actually. But I'll message Sam. Do you want her to be there, too?" Tommy asks.

"Probably wouldn't hurt if she can, just don't push her to come. She'll feel guilty if she already has something lined up. Sue was excited about this one and I want to make sure I'm not the only one trying to get her to consider settling in Greenstone. So as long as you are with me, maybe Bryant, Chuck, and Matt, too, we should be okay."

"Getting on Sue's good side, are you?" Tommy teases and I step through the front door with Courtney behind me in time to see Jackson playfully punch Tommy's arm.

"There you are Avery Jo!" I hear behind me. I'm wildly grateful that I wasn't a few steps closer to Jackson when Chuck decided to come down. He hops down the final few stairs and flings the door open and holds his arms out wide. "I haven't seen you, yet. Congrats."

And I'm completely enclosed in the third pair of Landen brother's arms in the last half hour. I've always loved how easy things were between our families. With Jackson and Chase being the oldest of each family, we all became comfortable with each other quickly.

"Thank you," I say, smiling up at him. "If it had been at all practical, I would have asked for you to fly me home."

"You do like to conveniently forget that you get wildly sick in the air."

"I'm convinced that's only because the pilot makes things extra bumpy when I go up."

"Uh-huh," he says, giving me one more squeeze.

Courtney has both of our bags and announces it's time for the ladies to head out. We wave to everyone. I do my best to not hug, or kiss, Jackson, but I feel him brush his fingers above my tattoo, whispering, "Later" as I walk by.

It's a good thing that only Courtney can see my face. I need to figure out how to not blush so much in front of everyone. But right now, I don't care.

The drive is fast and I park my truck in its usual spot before heading up to my very own office.

I hear someone coming up the stairs after about ten minutes of adding documents to two of my binders when Chase knocks on the doorframe.

"It looks like you're making progress."

"Well, someone gave me a ridiculously beautiful system to build on," I say honestly.

He smiles and looks around the room. "I know you rode Misty the other day, but I'll be stopping by Sunday to help Jackson saddle one of the stallions that gets spooked easily. Would you like to come with?"

I'm not going to say no to seeing Jackson.

"Sure, I'd love to sneak in another ride. Unless you two need an extra hand?"

"We'll be set, but you looked so refreshed and happy after the last time you rode Misty that it seemed silly not to ask."

Oh no, I can already feel my face getting warm. I turn my chair and pretend to search for something in my stack of printed papers.

"You're the best. What time should we leave?"

"Three?"

"Perfect," I confirm. "I'll be ready."

I let out a slow breath as his footsteps fade away and pray this isn't a disaster waiting to happen.

Chapter 44
Jackson

I put my phone away. I really can't decide if I should be smiling or burying my face in my hands. They're both on the way. Not just Chase. But Chase and Avery.

I start gathering Misty's tack so Avery can hop on and head out when they arrive in the next few minutes. We're all adults and I know we can hide things, but after having the past few days of being free to touch her when I want, and to look at her? This will definitely be a test.

Thankfully, grooming Misty calms my mind, so I dive right into our routine. Grabbing her brush, I run it over her body with my free hand trailing to make sure I didn't miss a sore or any dirt before I saddle her up. There's a rhythm to grooming this horse that I don't get with the others. Something about the touch that she loves. I automatically murmur what I'm doing to her, so she knows where I'm headed and how my body shifts around hers.

As usual, nothing new comes up for her and I put the brush away and grab the hoof pick and talk her through my progress when I hear two car doors close.

I have to remind myself to act natural and take a breath before moving to Misty's second hoof. I'm running my hand down her final leg, one of her back ones, when I hear their boots. I keep my motions smooth and my voice even. They both know to come into the space calmly and to listen for someone in a stall with a horse.

"Hey girl, it's just like the day we met, isn't it?" Chase says softly.

I let out a chuckle. "Except now, kicking me isn't high on her list, thankfully."

Chase puts a hand over his heart. "I believe the credit for her not kicking you that first day lies with yours truly."

Setting her hoof back down, I roll my eyes at my best friend as Avery comes into view looking just as beautiful as ever. I give her a nod that I hope passes as friendly and not madly-in-love before turning to take my gear out of the stall.

"Can I grab the saddle pad?" Avery asks.

"Of course. I'll bring her out with the steps if you want to put it on her."

She beams up at me. I have to remind myself that she's always excited to be hands-on with Misty.

"You want to start with the lightest saddle?" Chase asks, bringing me back into the moment of what we're doing this afternoon.

I nod. "Chet prepped everything over in the tack area before."

"Okay, I'll go talk to him to get him used to me again while you two get Misty set so Avery can ride. Being out of the city seems to have brought back a spark I didn't realize was missing in her."

I make a sound of agreement in my throat because if I open my mouth, I can't be certain something stupid won't fall out.

Hearing Chase talk to the stallion while I bring Misty out to where Avery is waiting just feels right.

Guilt pumps through my veins.

Avery and I keep everything per our usual interactions. Well, our fingers might brush a few times, but we're both careful with how we look at each other and our tone.

Time passes quickly and Avery is riding an eager Misty into the field.

I lead the stallion to the pen, letting him explore the space once more while Chase and I bring out the gear. We keep our conversation calm, just talking about Ava, the farm, and Daffodil. It's easy and natural.

I'm lucky enough to have four younger biological brothers; they're everything. But Chase is family even if we aren't connected by blood. We've been there for every major, and minor, event in our lives and we work seamlessly together even now.

"When does he head back? He's from out of state, right?" he asks.

"Yeah, it's about a four-hour drive for them, and the plan is for them to be able to bring him home in less than a month."

"Looks like he's gotten some of his confidence back."

"Definitely," I agree, watching the stallion walking around freely with just the saddle pad on to get comfortable.

"What happened to him?"

"It sounds like a branch fell on his back in a random accident while he was saddled, but his rider was stretching during a break," I say. "He was drinking from a stream when it happened, and it didn't cause anything more than a bruise in physical damage, but ever since that happened, he hasn't been able to handle being saddled."

"Damn."

"Yeah, so now it's time for his first big test," I say.

Chase nods and grabs the saddle, it's the proper size for the stallion, but it's extra light to help ease a horse into wearing one again. I click my tongue and approach the horse who lets me take his lead and guide him back to the mounting block where Chase is standing so it's easier for him to place the saddle on evenly and slowly. I stand so the stallion can clearly see me and so I'm less likely to take a hoof to the face if he decides to rear back as Chase talks through what he's doing.

If anyone else does this with me, it's usually Bryant or Matt, but I know how much Chase loves to be part of Landen Acres when his schedule allows, and he's really good at keeping horses calm. He claims the only reason Misty didn't kick me that first day was because he was the genius who decided to feed her a constant supply of sugar cubes. But I know it was him. It was his voice and his demeanor that kept her calm enough for me to check her over when she was known for kicking when people were at her back legs.

I watch him do the same thing now. No sugar cubes needed. Just his calm confidence and gentle touch, helping keep this horse centered even as Chase steps off the block to tighten the girth so the saddle doesn't move around. The stallion shivers and huffs out a few breaths, but otherwise, doesn't show signs of agitation.

We step outside of the pen and let him move as he pleases for a time, eventually trotting with the saddle in place. No one will attempt to ride him today; we'll save that for next week. For now, this is what he needs.

A second set of hooves announces Avery and Misty's return, drawing my attention away from the pen. Chase puts a hand on my shoulder saying, "Thank you, Jax, she needs this freedom."

And for a moment, I just hold my breath.

This is what things can be like. *This* is what I'm fighting for.

Chapter 45
Avery

Riding towards the pen, I see Jackson and Chase standing side by side watching the saddled stallion trot. My heart squeezes at the sight. They have so much brotherly love between them and have spent their lives being there for each other. Hopefully, we're doing the right thing.

Hopefully, they'll be brothers-in-law one day.

That thought sets my heart fluttering.

I can tell when Jackson hears our approach; his hat shifts as he moves his head and then he turns around. God, to think that one day I'll be riding home to him for good has me practically swooning.

I really need to get a grip at some point, but right now, I'm going to have to keep reminding myself that this is real.

He gives me one of those waves where he flicks two fingers to the side as he leans against the gate of the pen with his elbows resting on the top bar behind him. I give him a big smile before Chase turns around and then give them both a wave.

My heart feels full seeing them together, like always. My brother and his best friend. The man of my dreams, and the sibling who has always been there for me.

Misty is definitely ready to head into the stables after I gave her free rein in the fields. There's something so beautiful when I let her take over. I don't know that I'd be comfortable doing that with any other horse, but Misty is truly the best horse I've ever met and maybe one day soon, she'll be "ours." I can't stop the smile that spreads across my face at that thought.

"You two look like you had fun," Chase says when we're close.

"We did," I tell them, leaning forward to rub Misty's neck. I might notice Jackson appreciating the view. "She was amazing, as usual, and I think we're both worn out."

"Good, she needed to get rid of some energy," Jackson says, rubbing her nose.

Chase holds out his hand for the reins. "I'll head in with you while Jackson brings in the stallion. We'll get done fast together and when we need to brush down the stallion, we'll have all hands on deck in case he's feeling cranky."

Jackson and I both nod and I dismount before Chase leads Misty into the stables. She loves this part and she's always so eager to get to the grooming part of the process. Chase handles cleaning and conditioning the saddle, bridle, and pad, which means I get to brush her down.

Even as I bring Misty into her stall, I can hear Jackson quietly talking to the stallion as he leads it back into the stables. I set the stool next to Misty's side before grabbing the brush to remove any dirt, sweat, or salt that has accumulated on her during the ride. I'm pretty sure that all three of us love to brush Misty, but I've never been as comfortable doing this part on my own with other horses. She really has a different temperament and loves this process, as long as it's someone she trusts handling it.

The fact that she trusts me has always felt like a gift. I'm not sure why, because she was easy-going shortly after Jackson got her, but the full trust between a person and something as special as a horse is just incredible. Time passes quickly and Jackson and Chase are at the stall entrance as I'm wrapping up.

"I can handle the hooves," Jackson offers. "That way you two can head home for dinner."

"Don't you need to eat dinner, too?" I ask.

"Rebecca is coming to the main house and Matt's cooking Italian, so I'm set."

I won't pretend that I'm not a little jealous that another woman is having a full family dinner with the Landen brothers at the invitation of my secret boyfriend, but I don't think I let it show.

"Make sure you guys have flowers for her," Chase says.

"It's not a date, Chase. They're trying to get a vet to move to town, not marry one of them."

Jackson chuckles, likely over me trying to *not* be jealous while *definitely* being jealous.

"We'll make her feel at home without overwhelming her with proposals of our undying devotion. How's that?"

"Good enough," Chase replies, slapping Jackson on the shoulder and then turning to me. "Let's head out."

"I'll be right behind you."

I make a show of grabbing the brushes and the stool as Chase heads towards his truck. Jackson stays put but rests his forearm high on the stall opening, creating one sexy archway for me to walk under.

"Are you jealous, Avery Jo Barnett?" His voice is quiet, making sure that my brother can't overhear anything.

I'm not going to lie to him. "I know I have nothing to be jealous about."

"That's not an answer."

"No, it's not. But the full answer feels silly because I truly don't think that you're going to pull out a ring for someone anytime soon or–"

"What would be so wrong with that?" he asks as I tuck the stool in its spot and put the brushes away.

I roll my eyes. "Asking the vet to marry you?"

"No, pulling out a ring for someone."

I turn and look at him. He's dead serious. "Well, I think there's someone who wouldn't think that was silly at all."

He nods.

"You better get out there before your brother comes looking for you. I'll pick you up in a few hours," he says, kissing the top of my head as I make my way out of the stables.

"I'll meet you at the end of the drive at eight-thirty."

"Don't show up full," he calls after me.

"What?"

"Don't eat a huge dinner," he says evasively. "I'll have something for us."

I smile and nod, giving him a little wave. The sunlight hits my face and I shade my eyes as I walk over to the passenger door of Chase's truck, country music already playing.

"Okay, so, I have to ask. Caleb?"

I laugh, clicking my seatbelt into place. "Seriously? What is with this guy, that he has the whole town in a tizzy?"

"I mean, he gives the Landen brothers a run for their money in the looks department and he's fresh meat."

"He's not livestock," I say.

"No, but you saw how high his bid went."

I don't tell Chase that I did not, in fact, see the bidding for Caleb and that I went back to start flirting with Jackson. But I do know what the end results were and can do the math.

"Seems like this town was aching for a mysterious bull rider taking time off the circuit in a new town."

"You haven't answered my question," Chase reminds me.

"I don't think you asked one."

He rolls his eyes at me. After such a great afternoon, I don't want to lie to him, so I give him something real.

"I'm already happy," I say, smiling.

"You definitely look it. Must be all this country air getting back into your system." He rolls down the windows. "But I know you'd like to be with someone one day. You seem completely over Gary, why not see the guy everyone thinks you should end up with?"

"And by *everyone*, you mean the town gossips? Because beyond a few mentions that he moved in, no one I really care about has said a word otherwise."

"Fair enough. I was just curious."

"It's always okay to ask, Chase."

He nods and tosses his hat to the back seat. We ride with the wind blowing in our hair in companionable silence the rest of the way home.

Well, home for now.

Chapter 46
Jackson

S hit, I'm almost late for our dinner with Rebecca. Just in case everything goes long with the vet and my brothers, I want things ready for Avery, so I put the oven on low, grab the to-go-style aluminum pan, toss some tin foil on top, and pop it in. If nothing else, the house will smell fantastic.

I give Felix his dinner, put my boots and hat on, and head out the door. By the time I get to the house, all four of my brothers are hanging around the kitchen. Bryant is the only one helping Matt, the other two are just giving him grief while sneaking bites behind his back.

"Damn, I think Chuck said he'd be here only three minutes early!" calls out Matt. I roll my eyes. I'm usually a little early and don't cut things too close. Who wants to be late and have everyone watching you?

Chuck bows and starts on a cheesy acceptance speech, which is my cue to head upstairs. Unfortunately, I hear footsteps behind me.

"What are you doing? She'll be here any minute."

Thankfully, it's just Tommy.

"I just need to grab something for later tonight."

"Aw, man, I don't need to know about that."

"You think I'm snatching condoms from my brothers?" I turn and ask my now-blushing younger brother.

"Well, I'm the only other person in this house who knows why you're leaving by eight twenty-three."

"Fair point," I say, resuming my journey, clearly not shaking Tommy.

"So?"

I sigh. "I'm just grabbing something from Dad's old stuff that I didn't take with me before."

Our boots hitting the wood floor is the only sound as we make it to our father's old room. None of us have changed a thing about it after we donated his clothes. I head right for the top left drawer in his taller dresser. It opens with a small tug, just like always, and I reach to the back. My fingers find the box and close around it. There's no use trying to hide it from Tommy, he's as nosy as they come. Plus, he's my only brother who knows what's going on.

I close the drawer and hold my hand out with my palm up, showing him the box. He looks at the box, then at me, and back at the box.

"Really?" he asks.

I nod, swallowing hard.

"Okay," he says, pulling me into a hug that I return right away. This feels like the closest I'll ever be to sharing this moment with our dad.

We hear Chuck yelling that someone's driving up to the house and we head back downstairs. I pocket the small box with my phone so no one notices it.

As we reach the kitchen, I make sure that I tell Matt how amazing everything looks and smells. Even though he's in his twenties, I still haven't fully let go of being his guardian. It's hard to forget the scared seventeen year old who had just lost his dad and thought he might have to leave the only place he'd called home.

The dogs are barking from their outdoor kennel off to the side of the house and I let out a sharp whistle to quiet them when I go out to meet Rebecca. She gets out of her car with giant sunglasses on her face. Her brown hair is pulled back into a ponytail and she's got on a blue skirt that reaches her knees, a yellow tank top with a few necklaces, and a pair of worn cowboy boots.

"Are you Jackson?" she asks.

I nod. "You must be Rebecca," I say, holding out my hand to shake hers. "You made quite the impression on Sue Barnett."

She smiles at me as she puts her sunglasses on top of her head. "She is the sweetest woman ever! When she told me about this community, I have to say that I was thinking our meeting might have been fate."

"Come inside and we can talk about details. I hope you don't mind that all four of my brothers will be here. We all handle different things on the ranch and, hopefully, we'll be able to give you a decent idea of what things are like here and answer your questions." I don't add that I've just about maxed out what I'm comfortable with, but this is a great thing for our town and she seems genuine.

"Sounds great!"

She's enthusiastic without seeming over-the-top, so I can see why Sue liked her. I introduce her to each of my brothers as we all sit down. The salad gets passed around as Chuck tells Rebecca about Dr. Harris's old practice. She asks some good questions and seems relaxed. It feels weird that we're the ones she's first meeting with. She's going to support the town and the greater Greenstone area, but I suppose we're one of the biggest landowners and we have plenty of horses and cattle to keep her busy.

Tommy tells her about the numbers that Dr. Harris gave us for clientele, and then about the fundraiser.

"You must have some spectacular cowboys around here to raise that much just for a group date," she says, impressed.

Tommy blushes but doesn't tell her that the two of us were part of the auction.

I answer questions about the models we purchased for various equipment to replace what Dr. Harris left. Honestly, I get the feeling she's just gathering the details so she can do the job well versus feeling like she's sitting through an interview. Heck, I haven't seen her in action, but she seems knowledgeable and engages with all five of us, asking questions of Matt, getting Chuck to be somewhat humble, getting every stat she can out of Tommy, and even getting Bryant to say more than a few syllables.

Soon enough dinner, dessert, and another hour of talking about her background and I'm all but pacing, just itching to hop into my SUV. I've learned more facts about chickens than I ever have before by the time Rebecca leaves.

Tommy comes up beside me and says, "Whoa, boy, you don't want the vet to think you're following her. Let's not freak her out over you being eager to snatch up my best friend."

I look around us, worried that someone heard.

"Relax, they're being responsible and cleaning up from dinner. I'll tell them you have a hot date to get to." He winks at me.

I level my gaze at him, which doesn't phase him in the least right now. And then I nod at him, realizing that letting them think I'm hooking up with someone isn't that wild of a notion, even if things in that department really slowed down in the last year or so.

Rebecca's car makes its way down our driveway and out of sight when Tommy nudges me with his elbow and whispers, "What are you waiting for? Go get her."

I smile at him as I jog to my car, the engine already running.

Chapter 47
Avery

What the fuck do you pack for an overnight with your secret boyfriend? Am I supposed to bring pajamas? Will we even sleep?

Jesus, I'm overthinking things. I grab a small bag, toss in a pair of shorts that I sleep in sometimes and a tank top with clean underwear, a toothbrush, deodorant, and a hairbrush. That seems reasonable. Right? Zipping it up feels final, but I might not actually need to change at all...well, I might need to put this dress back on in the morning.

It's finally eight twenty-five. The note for my parents is already on my bed, just in case they happen to look for me, so I pop the bag onto my shoulder and head down the stairs. Both of my parents have sleep apnea, which means they're hooked up to their hoses all night, so I don't have to be too careful with the noise I make when leaving. But I will admit I'm nervous that I'll get caught. I'm a grown-ass woman and can go spend the night with Jackson if I want to, but they're still my parents and I've been seeing my past boyfriends from hours away. They don't know what I normally do.

I suppose that nothing about this is normal though. I'm careful with the screen door and when it doesn't slam, I smile as I practically skip down the steps. Who would have thought things would be here? After all these years of quietly trying to get over Jackson Landen, I get to spend the night with him.

And one day, hopefully soon, we won't be hiding a damn thing. I snicker when I hear an engine idling around the bend. He's early, of course. I jog the rest of the way until everything comes into view and I let out a little squeal of delight at the sight in front of me: Jackson leaning against the trunk of his SUV, arms crossed over his chest, one ankle hooked in front of the other with his eyes trained on me.

He doesn't wait for me to get there, but meets me halfway, pulling me into a bear hug, breathing me in for a moment. When I look up at him, he's already kissing me like we haven't seen each other in months. Damn, I love this man.

"Let's get out of here, baby," he says as he pulls back, taking my hand in his.

"Only if you insist."

"Oh, I do." He opens the passenger door for me, gently smacking my ass as I hop in and closing the door before I say anything. He winks at me as he crosses in front of the SUV and as he opens his door he simply says, "I couldn't help myself."

I grab him by the collar of his slightly frayed plaid shirt so I can kiss him once more. This one feels fast and furious with our tongues fighting for dominance. I'm ready to crawl into his lap right here in the front seat until he slows things down and puts the car in gear.

"You hungry?" he asks, putting his free hand on my thigh with my fingers fully entwined.

"What?"

"I told you not to eat a big dinner. So, are you hungry?"

I chuckle. "Food isn't exactly what my body is focused on right now, Jackson."

He licks his bottom lip. "Mine isn't either, but I do have something ready for you that I think you'll like."

"We'll see if you were able to find something to distract me from a night with you."

He just smirks at me and says, "We'll see, Avery Barnett."

Damn it, I've known this man long enough to know I won't get anything out of him. Instead of stewing, I switch gears to make the most of the short drive.

"Okay, what does your night normally look like?"

"You gave up fast."

"No, I just know when to pick my battles."

He smirks. "I'm usually home by nine most nights that I'm out with Chase or my brothers, or others." He shifts uncomfortably.

"Jackson, I'm fully aware of your history. We already talked through the only person I was jealous of. It's not like I've been celibate."

I watch Jackson's jaw tick and his hand tightens on the steering wheel.

"Oh, come on, babe, this isn't breaking news."

"Call me that again," he says, squeezing my thigh.

"What, 'babe'?" I say, casually.

He gives me a heated look and I pretend to not be affected. There is plenty of time for that soon.

"Now that we've established your favorite pet name, how about you tell me about your schedule?"

"Usually sleeping by ten and up by six for breakfast. I'm in the stables well before seven to water and feed the horses. What about you?"

"I'm not quite back on farm time, yet, so I usually wake up at eight. But I can adjust. For my co-op to work, I won't be meeting with anyone too long after dinner, so I could start switching back soon."

"Just not tonight," he says.

"Just not tonight," I agree. "I meant to ask how dinner went with Rebecca."

"Good. She was really confident but not arrogant. She made Matt blush over his good cooking, talked numbers with Tommy, got Bryant to speak, and Chuck to rein things in. So, I'd say she was pretty damn impressive."

Something inside me thinks I should be at least slightly jealous, but I shut that down immediately. "Sounds like my mom did well if she can manage all of that in one dinner."

"Yeah, I think she'll do fine here."

Greenstone will only benefit from getting a large animal vet settled sooner rather than later. If Rebecca was able to make it through a dinner with all five Landen brothers the way Jackson said, then she'll be able to hold her own, even with the crankier ranchers and farmers who are more stuck in their ways.

We reach the turn to Jackson's house and it's not long until it comes into view. The gravel crunches beneath the tires and he looks over at me and smiles. My heart aches because this is what I've been waiting, wishing, and hoping for.

Jackson parks in the detached garage. I realize that I haven't been inside here. It's pretty tidy, of course, and his four-wheeler is off to the left. There are tools hung up on the walls, a series of cabinets, shelves with lumber, table saws, and a whole lot more.

Everything looks well cared for and I'm already itching to use everything I see to make a raised garden bed.

Apparently, you can take the girl away from her family farm, but you can't take the instinct to grow things out of her. Or something like that.

My door opens and I feel like I've been caught with something I shouldn't have.

"See something you like?" he asks, nodding towards the lumber.

"I might have scoped out a thing or two for a future project," I reply.

"Take what you want, it's yours."

Instead of getting out of the car, I grab his face and his lips meet mine. I break the kiss because I can't hold in my smile. It's not as if I haven't had access to boards and tools. Hell, I built our raised beds after the boards of the last ones finally rotted. It's just that he doesn't hold back anything. I've watched him be open and generous with those he loves, but he's never had a partner to truly share his life with and I didn't know if that would be hard for him.

Apparently not.

"Come on, I have something in the oven."

"I'm still curious."

"I know." He smirks and takes my hand and grabs my bag.

I can hear Felix meowing at us as we walk up the steps onto the porch. Jackson lets go of my hand to pull open the screen door, using his body to keep it in place as he turns the knob of the wooden door, pushing it so it opens a crack. He motions for me to go first, making me suspicious. If he were Tommy or Courtney, I would think there might be a crowd of people waiting inside to surprise me, but I know it's just us. Well, Felix, too, who is sitting on top of a bookshelf.

I push the door all the way open and when I breathe in, I can't help squealing because I have the best boyfriend in the whole world.

Chapter 48
Jackson

A very makes a sound of pure delight. She turns back to look at me as I follow her into the house and set her bag down.

"You did not!" she exclaims, jumping into my arms.

"I might have a connection with the chef," I say, kicking off my boots and carrying her to the kitchen, setting her down on the counter. I grab a towel as I open the oven door and pull out the tray of honey barbeque chicken. When I take the lid off the top, she scoots closer and peers inside.

"Oh my God, you are the best human on the planet."

I smile at that compliment as she tries to grab a piece of meat without burning her fingers. I chuckle as I head to the fridge to take out the potato salad and tea, setting them on the other side of her. I grab two forks, handing her one so she can spare her fingers, pour two iced teas, and dig right in with her.

She takes one of the glasses and holds it up to me, waiting. I lift the other, keeping it a few inches away from hers.

"To our first night together," she says, clinking the glasses together.

"The first of many," I say before taking a sip.

Her freckles scrunch together from her full smile as she sets the glass down. She pulls me to her with her free hand so I'm nestled between her knees instead of off to the side, and then she dives back into the chicken, making sounds of pure contentment. Every now and then I kiss her or steal her forkful, but the time is quiet and it feels good. We'll have plenty of meals all around this house in the future, but this feels perfect for tonight.

"Am I supposed to save room for dessert?" she asks, halting her fork a few inches from her mouth.

"I only planned out my dessert."

She looks at me skeptically. "Jackson, are you telling me that you made a dessert that only you like?"

"I never said you'd be eating it."

Her eyes widen and I can feel myself smirk. I have plenty of plans for tonight and tasting her is right at the top of that list. I casually eat another bite of potato salad as she watches me.

"I think the rest of this would make great leftovers for lunch," she declares.

"Do you now?"

"I definitely do. Who doesn't like to have honey barbecue chicken for lunch?"

"Such a practical mind you have," I say as she puts the lid on the potato salad, scootches me away with a quick kiss, and hops down from the counter. She heads right to the second drawer down on the far side of the dishwasher, returning with a container and lid that will fit the remaining chicken.

I can't help myself, I'm like a bee drawn to pollen. I step right behind her and wrap my arms around her. She leans into me while she makes sure that she doesn't miss any of the chicken. She stacks the containers and turns in my arms.

"You put the glasses and forks in the dishwasher and I'll put everything into the fridge?"

I nod, kiss the top of her head, and take care of the dishes, absolutely loving how comfortable she is here. Avery has never been an overly shy person, but the ease in the ways she fits into my life, my house, heck, even my horse's life...it all tells me this was overdue. That I hadn't just put her on a pedestal for all these years because I was afraid to let someone in.

Truth is, I was afraid of losing the smallest hope that we could be together.

I feel her finger tracing along the top of my jeans as I shut the dishwasher. Even though I hate crowds, I've gotten pretty damn good at charming people and I might let a little of that side of me show.

"Are you in a hurry for something?" I ask, keeping a casual tone while running one hand up her arm.

"Hmmm, I can't think of anything," she says, tugging me against her by my belt loops. She closes her eyes as my fingers travel up the side of her neck. They rest along her chin as my thumb traces her bottom lip.

"It's a good thing that I can." I tilt her chin up as I lean down to kiss her once. When I stand up she opens her eyes, giving me a little frown. I wink at her and tilt my head toward the stairs. "Come on, I still need my dessert."

She blushes just a little bit, but her eyes blaze with confidence as I take her hand and lead her out of the kitchen. I get impatient so I turn around and lift her up so she can wrap her legs around my waist and my arms can hold her tight against me. "Much better," I tell her as she weaves her fingers together behind my head.

"I don't think I'm the only one in a hurry."

"Never said I wasn't," I say, running the tip of my nose along her ear. She leans forward enough so she can place soft kisses up my neck and nibbles on my ear when I reach the top of the stairs. If I wasn't hard already, this would have done it and now I'm aching to have her. I hate the fact my room isn't where the office is because I'd be there already, but I manage to not run the rest of the way to the door that's cracked open.

Avery seems to be too busy driving me crazy to notice that I've paused for a moment because this is the first time I've brought someone into my space. I know she already looked around and that was a big deal for me, but she's going to be the first and only other person to be in this bed with me.

With that thought, I fully close the door in case Felix decides to wander in and stride over to what's now *our* bed.

Chapter 49
Avery

Truly, only Jesse's honey barbeque chicken stands a chance at distracting me from time alone with this man. Actually, the only reason I was okay with being distracted was because Jackson was there with me, making contact, breathing me in. But now, well, it's time this man got what he's been wanting.

He lays me down gently, almost reverently, and I remember he's never brought *anyone* up here. At least not in his room. It feels like he saved this for me.

I hold his face in my hands as he has one knee on the bed, leaning over me. His eyes search mine as I rub my thumb along his cheek. He gives me a questioning look.

"I just love you, babe," I say.

He leans down and rubs his nose against mine. I unhook my ankles and use one to push against the leg that's kneeling, and he shifts us so he can press down on top of me as we start to explore each other. There's something so different about our time together now versus the barn. We're still limited by our schedule to get me back before five so I'm in my room before anyone wakes up, but something about this feels luxurious. Especially when Jackson slowly trails his hand down my side to hold my hip.

I run my fingers through his short hair, holding his face close to mine as our lips find their ever-increasing rhythm. We don't feel close enough, even though he's fully against me, I just need to feel *him*. My hands shift their way to his chest, finding the top button of his plaid shirt. All of his shirts, except for the one he wore at the auction, are well-worn and so damn soft that I know I'll be walking around in them regularly. He pushes his chest off mine to give me better access and I make quick work of the first few buttons. I decide that I'd rather be able to touch his bare chest and back and I gather the fabric at his waist and pull it up. He pauses our kissing just long enough to let me get one arm out and the shirt over his head. Instead of letting me finish the job, he leans back to jerk the offending garment off his arm and tosses it to the floor.

The thought of one lone shirt on the floor of Jackson's bedroom makes me giggle.

"Not the reaction I was expecting," he says, frowning and looking down at his chest.

"No, not you, babe. Just the fact that your room is now messy thanks to us."

He looks towards where he threw the shirt and then gives me a heated look. "If you're thinking I can't handle one shirt on my floor, then wait until you see how well I do with your dress next to it."

Both of his hands make their way from my knees up my thighs as he keeps eye contact with me. As he starts to push my dress upwards, he pauses his progress to cup my ass, smirking. "So perfect," he murmurs.

I push myself up on my elbows so he can get my dress past my shoulders before he puts one arm behind my back, holding me up, while pulling the fabric over my head and arms. Damn, he's strong.

Once he bunches up the dress and throws it off to the side, he cups my cheek with one hand and kisses me while pressing me back against the mattress. It should be funny, or even off-putting, but the fact that I can taste honey barbecue chicken and potato salad on him just makes me want him all the more. His tongue takes command and increases the intensity while his hand snakes behind my back to deftly unclasp my bra. Jackson makes quick work of getting it off of me and having the lacey thing join my dress somewhere on his floor. But this time, I don't giggle. Fingers find my nipple and start to tease and tweak it as I run my own up and down the taught muscles of his back.

His lips leave mine to follow an invisible trail down my body, making me shiver with anticipation. He gives my other breast attention with kisses and nips, but I can tell his mind is focused on just one thing and it's not long before those kisses shift to my stomach. With a feather-light touch, his fingers leave goosebumps as they leave my nipple on their way to grip my thigh.

Jackson lifts his head and looks up at me, right before he reaches my curls and gives me a devilish smile. In one smooth motion, his knees are on the floor and he's turned me sideways on the massive bed, removed my underwear, and draped my thighs over his shoulders. I'm pretty sure I squealed during the maneuver, but all thoughts leave my head the second he takes his first taste of me tonight and his eyes close as he makes a sound of pure bliss.

"God damn it, Avery, you taste so fucking good."

I don't have a chance to respond because his tongue is immediately on my clit and I feel one of his strong fingers stroking its way into me. I cry out as he expertly finds my G-spot, making me climb quickly towards a hard and fast orgasm. Jackson rumbles something, unable to stop licking me into oblivion, and the vibrations I feel are absolutely delicious.

I'm only moments away from coming and I can feel my muscles flexing. My back arches and Jackson adds another finger, filling me up and adding to the intensity that has me ready to burst. He does the same thing he did in the barn where he sucks on my clit while he's able to keep licking and I think I call out his name as I come. My body shudders and my orgasm rips through me as he doesn't let up, drawing out every ounce of pleasure until my spasms stop and I feel completely limp.

He allows my legs to drop from his shoulders as he kisses from the inside of my thigh to my tattoo, already sending fresh tingles through me. Standing up, he unbuckles his belt, the one with the buckle I got for him, pulls his phone out of his pocket, and takes off his pants.

"I have an alarm set, so we don't have to worry about anything," he says as he climbs back on the bed with his underwear on and even though I just came, I'm already craving more of him.

"Lose it all, Jackson Landen," I tell him, gesturing to his navy blue underwear which he promptly pushes over his very-turned-on dick, kicking them away from the bed. Even more for his floor to look cluttered with. Suddenly, I feel his arms scoop me up to place me in the center of the bed where he lays next to me, running his fingers over my abdomen. I bring him in for a kiss and instead of dinner, I now taste *me* on his tongue and by the way he moans into my mouth, I don't think he's close to being sated.

Chapter 50
Jackson

Avery makes needy sounds as her kisses start to have an almost-frantic edge to them and I know she's already getting ready for round two. She pushes me onto my back and she straddles my stomach. I can feel the evidence of everything we just did as she presses herself against me.

I'm definitely not going to make her wait longer than necessary.

Gripping her hips, I sit up and lift her so my tip is lined up with her entrance. There's no hesitation on her part as she lowers herself onto me, allowing me to fill her as her eyes flutter closed. She's more than ready to take me after her orgasm.

Fuck, she feels even better than I remember.

I trace her tattoo with my thumb and move my other hand to her chin so I can tip her face down and kiss her. When we came upstairs, she tasted like her favorite meal, but now she tastes like mine. I let out a growl of satisfaction and she starts moving, rocking so she's pressed against my chest, and my hand wanders from her chin, down her back all the way to her ass. God, she really is perfect for me in every fucking way.

I know this angle won't bring her the most pleasure, and I intend to have her moaning my name at least twice more before I come, so I reach down and start rubbing her swollen clit causing her to gasp. I devour the sound as I crush our mouths together and she starts to bounce harder, faster. Our bodies smack as everything becomes more frantic and her breathing becomes shorter, each inhale sharper as she's nearing another climax, making me even harder.

"Come on, baby. That's it, you're almost there."

She whimpers into my mouth as her fingernails dig into my skin and I increase the speed of my thumb and meet her halfway with every thrust.

"Jackson," she pants. "I'm going to—" She's cut off by a gasp and she's crying out with her head thrown back. I watch the look of ecstasy on her face as she rides me through her orgasm, milking me with her release. Each time she clamps down around my dick it feels like I'm in heaven. Every shudder rolls through my entire body as she falls forward against me as I lay down so she can rest on top of me.

We keep our hips locked together and I hold still, even through her aftershocks. I brush her hair off her cheek as she pants, tracing something on my chest with her fingertip. After a few moments, I know it's a heart and I smile, wrapping my arms around her.

"I love you, too," I whisper into her hair, which is spread up onto my shoulder. I can feel her smile against my chest. She tilts her face so she can press her lips to my skin while shifting her hips ever so slightly and I moan. The shift is making it almost impossible to hold still and just cuddle.

But then I feel her kiss change.

"Are you giving me a hickey?" I ask, looking down at a view that I will never get tired of. She's straddling me, keeping my dick buried inside of her, her ass is gorgeous, and my gaze follows the line of her bare back to where she's face-down on my chest, sucking on me to leave her mark.

She hums her response, still attentive to the task at hand.

"Take your time, baby. Fuck, write your name across my chest so everyone knows I'm yours." *Well, not everyone, not just yet.*

She finishes and looks up at me. "They will soon enough. But for now, this one's just for me and I'll have to make sure it doesn't disappear too quickly."

"Would you like me to have something that shows everyone I belong to only you?" I ask.

"I just want you to be you." She rolls her hips again, watching my face intently. "But don't think I haven't noticed that you still need some attention… because I think I'm going to lose my mind if you don't take me again."

She clenches tightly around my shaft and my eyes close for a second. When I open them, she's smirking at me and has a challenge in her eye.

"And how would you like to be taken, Avery Jo?" My voice drops into a rumble.

"Dealer's choice."

"I thought you weren't playing games," I say.

"I believe I said if there were any games, I was playing for keeps," she replies with pure confidence.

"Okay then, dealer's choice it is."

I sit up and the motion makes her take me all the way in. But instead of staying just like this, I get my fingers under her ass and lift her off of me. Avery is clearly about to protest but I crush my mouth onto hers, showing her that we're not done.

I just need a moment before I'll be even deeper and in a position where I can better rub against her G-spot. I set her on the bed next to me and say, "Rest your face on the pillow, baby."

Avery practically falls forward, sticking her plump ass into the air. As I approach from behind, I run my hand over one side before nudging her legs a little farther apart, opening her even more.

Fuck, she's soaked.

I look down at my raging erection and it's covered in both of her releases. The thought of adding my cum to all of this turns me on more.

"You tell me what you need," I say.

"I need you. Now."

"You're definitely ready," I say, pressing deep inside of her in one fluid thrust. She makes a choked sound of pleasure as I bury myself fully, feeling her squeeze me as if she's trying to hold me for a moment. As usual, I can't deny her anything, so I wait until she wiggles against me before moving again, loving that I get to take the time to learn each and every thing that makes her moan.

Chapter 51
Avery

I've heard talk about Jackson and his skills in the bedroom over the years. We're both fully aware that we've both been with plenty of people and that we'll just consider our past partners "practice." All I can think about right now is that practice has made this man fucking perfect.

With my face pressed into pillows that smell like him, I can feel the pleasure building for a third time and I already know he's going to make sure I come again before he's done. His big hands grip my hips as his thrusts come faster and harder. I'm pretty sure my cries don't actually sound like the word "yes" at this point, but he seems to know exactly what I want. My hands fist his sheets, and I can hear him telling me that I'm beautiful, perfect, and that he loves me.

I press against him to increase the intensity. Our bodies are making slightly obscene sounds, but our moans drown them out as we both climb toward that cliff. He leans forward and his fingers slide from my hip to my clit. I have no idea how I'm on the verge of orgasm number three already besides the fact that the man I've longed for, and lusted after, is free to touch me however he pleases.

I reach one hand back so I can hold his face closer to mine as I turn my head, feeling his breath against my cheek.

"You've got this, Avery," he says, nipping my ear and causing me to whimper as I feel things my toes curl. I just nod my head, panting something incoherent. "Come with me, please."

Jesus Christ, that sends me right over the edge. I cry out his name and my fingers clamp down in his hair, keeping him right at my ear. A moment later I hear him let out a low grunt as he keeps thrusting into me as waves of ecstasy roll through me and I'm flooded with warmth. His fingers slow when I begin twitching.

I'm just about to collapse when his arm wraps around from my hip to my opposite shoulder. He easily lifts me and uses his other hand to pull the sheets and comforter back before gently placing me down and curling himself around me, covering us up.

He trails soft, lazy kisses along my shoulder and neck. I tangle our fingers together and slip one foot between his calves, just needing to be as close as we can.

"I love you," I whisper, completely spent.

"I love you, too," he replies. "Sleep now."

He gives me a squeeze as he rests his head on the same pillow I'm using. As I drift off to sleep, I smile thinking about how huge this bed is, and that we only need a sliver of it.

Chimes getting progressively louder wake me well before the sun has risen. My cheek is pressed against a chest that vibrates when Jackson grumbles something about hating his phone, but neither of us moves to turn it off.

In fact, his arms tighten around me, keeping me right on top of him, completely naked, of course. I don't remember sprawling across my boyfriend but I'm grateful I got to wake up like this because he's warm, soft, and apparently loves to cuddle.

Maybe not everything is soft.

I'm reminded of what we did before Jackson tucked me against him and realize there's no way I can go home reeking of sex. He must feel me tense because those arms hold me more securely.

"I set it plenty early," he mumbles into my hair, taking a deep breath in.

"So I have time for a shower?" I ask.

"And breakfast, but you have to release me so I can make it."

"Are you telling me that you're going to go downstairs at three-something in the morning to make us breakfast while I shower before you drive me back to Barnett Farms like a thief in the night?"

He mock-glares at me. "There were far too many words in that sentence for this early in the morning."

I scooch myself up his chest so I can kiss him. I'm sure my breath is terrible at this point, and I make a mental note to bring my bag all the way upstairs next time.

Jackson's lips are soft and his kiss is slow and almost lazy, like we could just lie here all morning rather than rushing to make sure I'm back in my bedroom well before anyone on the farm is awake.

"The water gets really hot, so check the temp before you get into the shower, and the green toothbrush is yours.

"What?"

"The water's hot, the green toothbrush is yours."

"You got me a green toothbrush?" I ask.

"I figured bringing one back and forth will get old, so yeah." He nips the tip of my nose before adding, "Plus, I might have had a hard time getting the green dress you wore the day you came back out of my head."

"You got me a toothbrush." I don't know why but my heart is a puddle of goo at the thought of Jackson at the grocery store looking at the toothbrush options and picking a green one for me. A green one because I wore a green dress the day of the auction after Tommy told me I'd have to make it obvious I was giving Jackson the green light.

His smile is soft as he looks into my eyes. He might not fully understand why this is so sweet to me, but he clearly knows I'm having a moment.

Tucking my hair behind my ear, he says, "I got you a toothbrush. But you have to bring whatever shampoo you use because if my pillows don't start smelling like peaches soon, I might lose my mind."

"How'd you know I use peach shampoo now?" I ask.

He raises one eyebrow. "Must be one of my many talents."

I roll my eyes before I kiss him. It's just an easy, gentle kiss. Nothing frantic, just comfortable and safe. As crazy as it sounds, I feel completely at home right now. This is only the second time I've even been in this room, but the fact that Jackson built it and that he's here tangled up with me makes me feel grounded.

I feel him squeeze my ass as he says, "We need to get out of this bed now, otherwise, I'm keeping you here forever and everyone will wonder why I'm neglecting the ranch."

"Alright," I say, begrudgingly sitting up. "I'll go shower so Misty doesn't miss her breakfast."

"Even the horses don't eat this early. Do you still like your eggs over-easy?" he asks.

"We haven't had breakfast around each other for years."

"I've been paying attention for quite some time," he replies, shrugging.

"Well, I'll just have to show you what I've observed as well. But, yes, I do like my eggs over-easy."

He nods as if he just wrote the order down and then places a hand on my cheek. Our gazes stay locked on each other.

"I Iove you."

"I love you, too, babe."

Chapter 52
Jackson

I have orange juice out already, the bacon is crisp, just the way she likes it, and I'm cracking the fifth egg into the skillet when I hear her walking towards the stairs. Damn, it feels amazing to have her here, even if it's an ungodly hour to be awake.

Felix continues to give me the side-eye from his bed near the cubbies, likely deciding if bacon is worth getting up for. Avery scratches him under his chin, wearing her dress from last night, and drops her bra in her bag. I abandon the eggs for a moment to scoop her up with a kiss to place her right where she was last night on the counter. She tastes like my toothpaste and smells like my body wash.

"If I didn't love your peach shampoo so much, I might ask you to switch to only using my products," I say between trailing kissing down her neck.

"I can mix things up," she replies, "especially if it has you greeting me like this."

I pull back to look at her. "Baby, how you smell has nothing to do with how I greet you, it's just a bonus."

Her cheeks flush and I give a quick kiss right on her mouth. I hand her a piece of bacon as I flip the eggs. She gives it a thoughtful look and the corner of her mouth rises before she takes a bite.

"I could get used to this, you know."

"You better," I say, plating the eggs. I pass her the plate with two eggs and set the one with three on the counter right next to her, standing between her legs while cutting up my eggs.

"Does this mean we're never going to use the table?" she asks.

"Not unless you're sitting on my lap."

She laughs, likely assuming I'm at least partially joking, and pulls me in for a kiss. I swear I can't get enough of this woman.

I hesitate a moment before I reach into my front pocket, past my phone, and pull out the box I grabbed from the main house. Avery drops her fork onto her plate as her eyes take in the box and immediately find mine.

I clear my throat.

"I just want to be clear where I am." I turn the box over in my fingers, looking down at it for a moment. "This was my grandmother's and she left it for me. My dad held onto it and until you came back, I never thought I'd use it. If it's not a great fit, it's easy to get it resized if you decide you want it for your wedding band."

My cheeks are burning right now, I didn't mean to blurt that part out, so I keep rambling.

"But if you want something else, something new that's just for you, I have ideas for that, too. You don't have to open it or do anything with this." I awkwardly wave the box between us as she stays silent, likely still watching me, but my brain feels like it's all jumbled up because I'm afraid all of this was too soon and she's going to run for the hills. "I just wanted you to know. And I fully intend to talk to your family, I'm not sure if you'd like me to ask their permission, I get the feeling you're not fond of that tradition, but I want them to know how I feel, I'll wait until you're ready."

I wince at how awkward that was and chance a peek at her. She has tears flowing down her cheeks and when our eyes lock, she just nods and breathes one word: *yes.*

Breakfast goes too quickly and before I know it, I'm pulling up to the bend in the driveway to her parents' house. I shift into park and pull our joined hands up to my lips so I can kiss her knuckles, one at a time.

"I do have to leave your SUV to, you know, sneak back into the house."

"Fine," I relent, releasing her hand so I can say goodbye to Avery outside.

I cross in front of the bright headlights as she's closing the passenger door. Her bag drops to the ground and her arms wrap around my neck as she makes a sound of delight when I start to bend over, running my hands over her ass to pick her up. God damn it, she feels incredible.

I stand and press her against the passenger door as her feet hook together behind my back. At the house, she told me she wanted the box and then she kissed me like I was the other half of her soul. I'm keeping the ring inside the box until it's time to share that part of the news with our families. But she's mine and I'm hers, and in two weeks, we'll tell Chase and go public with the fact that we're dating so he doesn't worry that we've rushed into this without thinking things through.

She looks into my eyes and says, "I love you," before pulling my face to hers in a bruising kiss, not letting me up for air. Our mouths move perfectly together and when my tongue darts past her lips, she makes one of those whimpering sounds in the back of her throat that drive me crazy. I have half a mind to open the back door so I can lay her across the seats and have her crying out my name. But I had that just a few hours ago and I'll have it again. For now, we'll make the most of these moments that we carve out just for us.

"Put. Her. Down."

Fuck, I'd know that voice anywhere.

Avery holds tight against my neck and I hear her whisper, "No, no, no, no, no."

I give her a squeeze and loosen my grip.

"Now." Chase's voice is unsteady with rage. Shit. He's only been this pissed one other time.

God damn it, this couldn't be more of a disaster. Avery unhooks her feet but keeps her eyes closed. If only it were that easy to make this anything but the waking nightmare it is.

"Chase," I say as I slowly turn around.

"No." He cuts me off with one sharp word. Shit. I shouldn't have turned around. He's redder than I've ever seen him with his fists shaking at his sides.

"It's not—" Avery starts and stops when he shoots her a look and takes a step towards us.

I might be an idiot, but I automatically step in front of her so Chase is confronting only me. I'm the one who's been the problem all these years. In his mind, she just succumbed to my charm. I'll play the villain if it stops something from breaking between them.

I hold out a hand, trying to placate him. "I promise you—"

A split-second later my cheek is on fire. Avery screams and pushes me behind her. Fuck. Didn't think he'd take a swing so soon.

"Chase are you out of your fucking mind?" Somehow Avery is mostly blocking me from his view.

"Whatever promises he tries to make mean jack shit now. Move, Avery."

"What, are you going to hit me too if I don't?"

I see him pause.

"Yeah, that's right, you just hit your best fucking friend—"

"No," he tries to interrupt.

"—in the whole world and now you get to go through me."

I stand up to my full height, my left eye already swelling shut and I look at him. Under all the fury, I see the pain.

"Get the fuck out of here."

I can hear Avery shouting at him but everything is starting to sound fuzzy. Fuck. I take a breath and hold my hands up by my chest, walk around the front of my SUV, and get in the driver's seat. Shifting the car into reverse, I look up at the woman of my dreams who has tears streaming down her face. She gives me a nod and I dip my chin before backing down their long driveway.

It's not until I catch a glimpse of myself in the rearview mirror that I realize I'm crying, too.

Chapter 53
Avery

I attempt to take a steadying breath as I watch Jackson's SUV drive away. I know he's not leaving me. I know this. But my heart feels torn to bits from this whole ordeal, all the same.

And then I turn back to the asshat of the year recipient.

"Are you serious?" I throw my arm out toward the dust trail.

"Are *you* serious?" he counters.

"Not only did you apparently think it was okay to hit someone, you just kicked your best friend off the property like you own the damn place!"

"I had no choice, Avery," he says, fuming, "and he's not the only one that should leave."

"What the fuck?"

"You knew, Avery, you *knew* that fucking my best friend would make me cut you both out."

"Oh, I made you do absolutely nothing, you're just blinded by some preconceived assumption you've made about two people who love you and have been trying to *not* hurt you."

"And here I thought you were the smart one." He practically sneers at me and turns around.

Oh hell no.

"Chase Martin Barnett, you do *not* get to walk away from me." Curse my short legs.

He storms down the path leading to the carriage house.

"Jesus Christ, Chase, can you take your head out of your own ass for two full seconds and listen to me?" I'm jogging now, holding my boobs because my bra is in my bag, which I completely forgot about the second Chase saw us.

"When the fuck did you stop respecting that I get to make my own goddamn choices?" I throw at him.

He stops in his tracks and turns on me. Thank God. I'll take him screaming at me over him shutting down.

"Me?" He laughs bitterly. "That's rich coming from you. You just had to go and be with the *one guy* who is guaranteed to *shatter* your heart, which will then make me lose my best goddamn friend in the world because I can't handle being around anyone who fucks with my family and you know it."

"Listen to yourself. Just listen."

"Listen to what, Avery. Huh? Should I listen to the fact that I know Jax better than anyone else in this entire world? I love him like a brother, I really do, but when you love someone, you know them. You know their strengths and you know their flaws. And he has a pretty huge one when it comes to dating: he's incapable of letting anyone in. He won't and he can't, Avery. If you refuse to see that, then I'm done. You can get the hell out of here, too."

"Chase, just *stop!*" I yell, letting all the bottled up frustration that has been building with him explode. "Have you ever *once* asked your best fucking friend *why*? Have you ever stopped to look with your own two eyes at what has been holding him back from giving his heart to someone? No. Because your need to first protect Susan and then *me* from heartache trumped both his happiness and mine. So get your head out of your fucking ass and apologize to your goddamn best friend and stop being an overbearing piece of shit best friend and brother."

He just stares at me and before he lays into me again, I turn on my heel and stomp back to the house to pack a bag and get in my truck without one glance back.

It doesn't take long to grab my things and leave a note for my parents. I somehow kept most of my tears from it though, but I can't have them mediate this. Chase is too far gone right now to reach. Plus, Ava needs him calm so I can't be around pissing him off several times a day just by being on the farm.

I try Jackson's phone twice but he doesn't answer. Shit. My jacked-up nerves right now have me on the edge of panicking, but he might need time to process.

That's all.

Right?

Fuck. Now I'm paranoid that the only thing he's doing right now is deciding how to let me down gently.

No. That's not Jackson. That's who Chase believes Jackson to be, but that's not him. That's not *my* Jackson. And he sure the hell is mine.

Courtney won't be awake for several more hours, but my other bestie will be soon. Before I pull onto the highway, I send Tommy "SOS" and my phone rings almost immediately.

"You okay?" Tommy asks.

"No," I say, trying not to sob while driving.

"I'm grabbing my keys and will be there in a few minutes, are you at home?"

Home. That word has too many meanings for me now.

"No, can I come to you?" I manage to say without losing it.

"Of course. Wine, coffee, or tea?" he asks.

"All of the above," I say with a teary smile. Leave it to Tommy to think of something like beverage choice when I'm having a meltdown.

"They'll be ready when you get here. Drive safe."

I hang up and do my best to not hear the sound of my brother punching the man I'm head-over-heels in love with.

I fail miserably, but I only have to pull over once on the short drive to Landen Acres to let myself scream through my tears until my eyes are clear enough to see. Tommy is on the porch, wearing a long-sleeve tee and setting down two steaming mugs when I pull in. When he jogs over to my truck, I throw it in park, stumble out the door, and fall apart in his arms.

Tommy holds me tight for a moment before pulling back and looking me over with a panicked look in his eyes.

"No," I say, "no one hurt me like that."

"Thank God," Tommy breathes and pulls me right back into his arms, resting his cheek on the top of my head.

He lets me cry against his chest until I can breathe normally enough to whisper, "He saw us."

"Fuck, I'm sorry, Avery." Tommy kisses the top of my head.

"He hit Jackson." Tommy tenses, likely debating staying with me, hitting my brother, or tracking down Jackson. I wipe my nose with the back of my sleeve as he steps back, keeping his hands on my shoulders.

Tommy's eyes look murderous. "Did he hit you?"

"No." I understand why he's double checking, though.

Tommy nods, puts an arm around me, and says, "Let's go to the porch. I only prepped the tea, but it has plenty of honey and whiskey in it."

"Thank you."

"You never have to thank your best friend and you know that." He squeezes me against him and we grab my bags and head to the porch.

Chapter 54
Jackson

*F*uck.

I keep wracking my brain for what we could have done differently, but how could we have guessed that Chase might be out for a stroll at four in the morning?

My eye is almost swollen completely shut and I'm grateful Chase isn't left-handed, or I'd have a cut from his wedding band to boot. The same wedding band I carried the day he married Ava. The day I stood next to him as a brother by choice. My entire chest hurts from trying to catch my breath.

Instead of icing my face like I should have, I went straight for saddling up Misty because riding is what centers me when shit hits the fan. So here I am, likely letting my cheek and eye get worse while I give Misty free rein to bring us wherever she pleases, and she wants to run this morning, so we're covering ground fast. All while I try to let everything out.

She finally slows down where the trees are closer together. I know she's headed right for the creek that's just on the other side of this small hill. She trots down, breathing hard from her run, and from carrying me, and before she gets to the running water, I give the reins a gentle tug while murmuring a soft, "Whoa, girl."

She comes to a stop right away and I swing my leg over and hop down, pulling the reins over her head so I can walk with her. She nudges me with her nose after a few steps and I rub her chin. My mind is all over the place.

When we reach the stream's edge, I squat next to her and splash my face with the cold, clear water. Both of my eyes feel relief. One is swollen from my best friend's fist, and the other from crying.

The sun is starting to rise and I wonder if it's okay to call Avery. If she and Chase are talking, I don't want to mess things up by reminding him that he just caught us with her legs wrapped around me.

My heart fractures more as my mind replays the hurt that radiated off of him. I went and did the one and only thing he has ever asked me not to do. Chase has been a brother to me. He's seen me and cared for me in ways that my own flesh and blood couldn't at times. And I'm the bastard who couldn't trust him with the truth. Shit, I've been in love with Avery, and known about it, for over five years. How much of an asshole am I that I couldn't just tell him? Especially if she was dating someone else. Then it would have just been a confession that I clearly wasn't going to do anything about. But no, I couldn't even do that for the person who has been there for me through everything.

I know I can't fix things between us right now, but I can't let everything fall apart between Avery and Chase. He's pissed at me. I'm the older one in this relationship who promised, time and time again, to not be with either of his sisters. My brain is all over the place and I can't slow it down.

God damn, I just want to see Avery and know that she's okay. Shaking off my hands, I reach for my phone, hoping I haven't missed a call from her, and hoping that I've heard something.

I pat my front pockets, noticing they're empty. I let out a frustrated groan that causes Misty to look my way.

Fuck, I set my phone on the ledge in Misty's stall in case Avery called while I was getting Misty set for our ride. I have no idea why that made sense at the time, but having to dig my phone out of my pocket while it was ringing felt like too much in those moments and then I fucking forgot to grab it.

Misty is done drinking so I flip her reins back over her head and step into the stirrup.

"You ready to head back, girl?" I ask, rubbing the side of her neck. She gives her head a little shake and stomps her front hoof with impatience. "Alright, let's go."

She gallops the whole way, but instead of going to her stable, she veers to the closer one next to the main house. I'm about to correct her, anxious to get my phone, but then I see Avery's truck parked haphazardly in the driveway.

My heart is thundering in my chest and I urge Misty on, pressing my hat down as she flies over the field of grass around the main house. As we approach, I can see two people curled up together on the bench. Tommy holds up a hand so we're quiet and it looks like Avery might have fallen asleep. I get down and tie Misty up under a tree near the house, jogging the rest of the way to the porch.

Tommy puts one finger to his lips. Avery's eyes have red rings around them, but they're closed and her breathing is even. He nods to the two suitcases I hadn't noticed on the porch and looks at me expectantly.

I tilt my head to her car and whisper, "Keys inside?"

Tommy nods once more and I grab both suitcases and put them right in the bed of Avery's truck. I turn around and head back up the steps to the porch and scoop Avery up in my arms. She makes a soft sound and relaxes against me immediately.

"Go. She cried herself to sleep a little while ago," Tommy whispers. "I've got Misty and will do the morning rounds."

"Thank you."

He gives me a sad smile and I turn around, carrying Avery to the passenger side of her truck. Once I get the door open, I recline the seat for her and lay her down. Again, she barely stirs.

"Let's get you home, baby," I whisper as I kiss her cheek. I quietly shut her door, get in the driver's side after moving the seat all the way back, and turn on the ignition.

I sigh and put the truck in gear, heading home with the woman I love and my heart torn in two.

Chapter 55
Avery

I stir a little. My eyes are crusted shut, I feel like I could drink a gallon of water, and my head is pounding from crying so much. My hair feels matted against the side of my face, but it's dry, so it's been a while since I took my shower at Jackson's, so I have no clue what time it is.

There's a heavy arm wrapped around my waist and a warm chest pressed against my back. I smell Jackson's sweat mixed with the leather of his saddle and a little bit of Misty.

Before rubbing my eyes and seeing whatever this hellish day has to offer, I trace my fingers up his forearm until his hand fully envelops mine. Honestly, I have no idea how I got here. The last thing I remember was crying into Tommy's chest as I told him what happened.

"Hey." His voice is hoarse, like he's been screaming or sobbing just like me. His nose rubs along the back of my neck.

"Hey," I whisper, not trusting my voice just yet. I squeeze my eyes tight and use my free hand to rub them and wipe everything away.

I bolt upright, causing him to sit up, holding my face and telling me that things are okay.

"How are things okay?" I ask, feeling the tears building. My fingertips ever so lightly touch his already-bruising eye, which is almost swollen shut. "Have you iced this?"

"No. I probably should've, but it might be a little late to avoid a mark."

I know he's trying to lighten the mood, but my heart breaks seeing him like this.

It's all my fault.

"I'm sorry, babe." Leaning in, I kiss his forehead close to the swelling, but not where it should be sensitive. "I'm so sorry."

"Nothing was your fault. You have absolutely nothing to be sorry about." He guides me so we're laying down and I'm tucked against his side while he's on his back. This isn't a battle I'm going to win right now so I nod against his chest.

"I wasn't sure what to think when I didn't hear back from you."

"I definitely get to apologize for any added stress that gave you. My phone's in Misty's stall."

"Why?"

"I didn't want to miss a call if you needed something, so I set it off to the side while getting Misty's saddle on her and everything was so jumbled in my head that I didn't realize I left it there until Misty stopped for water. I didn't want to bother you or make things worse if you were still talking with…" His voice chokes up.

"Yeah, I get that." As I look out the window, it finally registers in my head that it's clearly well-past when Jackson should be up and with the horses.

"Wait," I say. "Who's feeding the horses if you're here with me?"

"Tommy." He squeezes me. "I kept thinking you were taking some time and space, so I took Misty out to try to clear my head.

When I realized I didn't have my phone, we turned around and she led me to you."

"She knew," I say, tracing a heart on his chest as he kisses the top of my head while he nods.

We stay like this for a little minute, just holding on and putting a few pieces of our broken hearts back together.

"Should we try to do something a little normal today?" he asks.

I let that sink in. It might be a good idea so I don't stew all day, and work is never really done on the ranch.

"I grabbed my binders, I can set things up in the office."

"And schedule a meeting with Tommy and Sam. He has the numbers not only from the auction but other fundraisers and community events for her and the three of you can strategize about your secret co-op."

"After another moment of this."

His arms continue to hold me close and we just lie there tangled up together. My head lifts with each of his breaths and after this morning's shit show that we still need to process, being able to ground myself in his embrace feels like a gift.

Every so often he kisses the top of my head, and sometimes I feel a stray tear to wipe from my cheek. We whisper that we love each other. But I think we both need this quiet contact. We need to know that we're truly in this together. We need to know that we didn't just fuck everything up. We need to know that when the dust finally settles, that we belong to each other.

Jackson's stomach growls and I feel the vibration against my torso.

"Leftovers?" I ask, looking up at him. One corner of his mouth lifts and he gives a little nod. "You shower this time, I'll get things ready downstairs."

He crooks one finger, tucks it under my chin, and holds me in place as his mouth finds mine in a slow and borderline desperate kiss. Our breathing is loud through our stuffy noses from crying this morning. My hand reaches up to cling to the back of his neck, keeping him there with me, deepening our connection and commitment. His response is immediate, his mouth parting and his tongue tracing my lower lip. A desperate squeak escapes me, which he hungrily consumes before he slows things down.

My eyes open and take in his swollen face, my heart breaking again.

"We need to get something on this, babe."

"Yeah." He sighs, running a hand down my back. "I'll clean up first and meet you downstairs."

I kiss his forehead and crawl over a still-laying Jackson, grabbing my phone which is charging on the nearest table. Plenty of missed calls and messages from my parents, Tommy, Courtney, Ava, and even Susan. But not Chase. No surprise.

Looking around the room, I pause.

"Your suitcases are in your truck. I wasn't leaving you for a second."

It's like he reads my mind. I turn around and give him one more kiss, carefully holding his face in my hands. "Thank you."

"You never have to thank me, baby."

Chapter 56
Jackson

Being with her feels like being in the eye of a tornado: a perfect calm right where you are in that moment, while a storm rages around you. She's my rock, my calm, my everything.

I look in the mirror to see my bruise yellowing around the edges. It's about damn time. This thing has been purple, black, and a little green for a week now and every time Avery looks at me I feel the guilt radiating from her. It doesn't matter what I say to her, it's still there.

And I hate it.

I'm so pissed at myself for getting carried away with her when I should have kept my fucking hands to myself as I dropped her off. I knew it was risky to take her all the way to the bend in their driveway, but the thought of her walking half a mile in the dark was out of the question.

If only I could have let her open her own damn door and driven away, we might have just missed him.

But no. I had to have her to myself just a little bit longer and now Chase isn't responding to a single message or phone call from either of us. He opens them so we can see they're read and that's it.

My mind replays coming home for lunch two days ago when I could hear the end of Avery's conversation with Ava. Avery in tears while making sandwiches for us as Ava told her Chase is miserable but that he's still hurting so not to expect anything just yet. Me silently walking up to Avery and taking her into my arms as they finish their conversation and letting her cry against my raw heart.

I keep promising her that things will be alright again. That she'll have her brother back, and I'll have my best friend back. I'm just losing my ability to wait. My pain is something I can deal with, I can give Chase more space. But Avery's broken heart is something I can't handle for much longer without losing my mind. I've never felt so helpless.

The shower turns off and Avery's arm snakes out, grabbing her towel from the hook. A few moments later, she steps out, tucking the end of the towel in so it's wrapped around her curves. Her hair hangs wet down her back and I can't stop myself from tucking a stray strand behind her ear and ducking down to kiss her.

"When do you leave?" I ask.

"In about an hour."

"Want to take the four-wheeler?"

She laughs. "I think I'm going to drive my truck in case it rains. Gotta keep the binders dry, you know."

"Can I do anything before I head out for errands?"

"Thank you, babe, but I have it all set. I'll see you for lunch though, right?"

I kiss her again and hum my *mmhmm* before leaving the bedroom.

"Don't forget the chocolate!" she calls after me.

"I wouldn't get cookies tonight if I didn't have it on my list," I call back as I duck into the office and make my way downstairs.

Stepping into my boots, I give Felix a scratch behind the ears, much to his delight. He stretches so I continue down his back as he purrs and curls back up on his place in the sun.

My nerves build in my gut as I grab my keys and hat. I pause on my porch to take a few deep breaths in an attempt to find a little calm. The smell of nearby stables, the muted sounds of horses neighing, and the feel of a light breeze grounds me in this moment and not what may come.

Stepping off the porch, I make my way to the garage, unable to feel a certain amount of satisfaction at seeing Avery's truck next to my SUV.

The ignition hums as I remind myself why I'm pushing and I hightail it out of here.

Chapter 57
Avery

I hear the front door close as Jackson heads into town to run errands while wrapping my hair in a towel and continue getting ready. I'm bringing a small batch of peanut butter cookies that are currently cooling. Sam and I have barely had a chance to cross paths since she moved here, but I really don't want her to feel any of the jealousy that used to burn in me. Heck, even if they really dated, I had no claim on Jackson at that time.

But that was then, and this is now. Sam's job is to literally help the town thrive and I think we have a fighting chance to come together and bring the farmers and ranchers into the fold.

I grab the sundress hanging closest to Jackson's shirts and get dressed. I take a moment to appreciate how easy living with Jackson has been. With all the turmoil I feel about how and when Chase found out about us, at least this has just reinforced that we're not crazy and impulsive.

Once I'm ready, I pile the cookies into a tall container that's just the right size to hold a stack of ten and put the cooling rack that I bought into the dishwasher, flipping around the plates Jackson loaded after breakfast. Looking at the clock above the sink, I see I'll be plenty early, but I can easily keep myself busy at the main house.

I grab the cookies and head over to my boots and the tote I loaded up last night as my phone rings.

"Hey, Tommy, I'm just ready to leave, I hope that's okay."

"Are you still at the house?" he asks.

"Once more, it's lovely to chat with you, too," I tease. "And yes, I am."

"You know I love you to death and we don't need to bother with pleasantries at this point."

Fair enough.

"Can you grab a folder that Jackson took back with him last week?"

"Sure, what is it?"

"It's Dr. Harris' stud records, he had the most accurate ones for which horses were bred or not for the area and we've had more requests than usual for a few of ours."

"Don't you have your own records?" I ask, walking up the stairs to the office.

"Of course we do," he replies in mock-offense. "But I want to cross-reference closer relatives of our studs to make sure we're not inbreeding."

"Wouldn't want that."

"Nope."

In the office now, I go right to the filing cabinet and open the top drawer, working my way alphabetically through the tabs that Jackson so neatly organizes until I get to the H section.

"We have one that says 'Horse Lines' and one that says 'Studs' in Harris' files. Which one do you want?"

"Oooh, I forgot that Harris had two tracking systems, bring them both, please." Tommy sounds like a kid in a candy store knowing that he's about to immerse himself in data.

"Can do, I'll see you soon."

"See ya."

The top drawer closes funny sometimes, so I set my phone and the two folders down on the desk which now has two chairs with Jackson's computer off to the left instead of the center. I fiddle with the latch for a moment before getting the drawer shut and turn to pick up my things.

Something's different.

I look around the desk as my stomach clenches without my consent. I know there's no reason to think anything's wrong. Jackson hasn't given me a reason to doubt him and I'm not starting now.

It's just hard to not wonder where the box went with his grandmother's ring inside...my ring.

Chapter 58
Jackson

By the time I turn off the highway, my palms are sweaty, making the leather on my steering wheel feel sticky. I'm trying to be confident going into this because I know exactly what I want and now that I have it, letting it go really isn't an option. But when I replay the events of one week ago, my gut churns and I question the decision to come here so soon.

But if anyone knows Chase Barnett as well as me, it's the woman he married. Ava is the one who helped me plan out the timing for my visit so I'm showing up not only during a break in Chase's work routine, but when his mood was more forgiving before we went out in the fields. I'm going to trust her instinct that I'm not making things worse.

As I approach the bend where shit hit the fan, my eye twitches involuntary and a fresh wave of guilt washes over me. I drive right past the last spot with enough space to turn my SUV around, staying left at the turn for the Barnett main house, and hear Daffodil's bark before seeing the former carriage house that Chase and Ava converted into their home.

Chase sits on the porch steps, elbows resting on his knees and picking the dirt and grime from his fingernails. He's in his well-worn jeans with work boots and t-shirt with the sleeves torn off.

He definitely just came in from the field.

I've seen him just like this thousands of times. Today is just so different. It's not like we never fight. We do. But I don't quite know where to look, and neither does he. I park and make my way to the other side of the steps, steps that I know well, petting Daffodil who seems to be less on guard since the last time I was here.

"She's calmer." I'd rather break the ice with something neutral, even if I want to grimace at how forced my voice sounds.

Chase reaches out and Daffodil accepts the scratches while her tail thumps against his leg. "Yeah, she's close to her normal self."

I nod and we sit there for a moment, Chase petting his dog and me looking out at the trees that line the driveway.

"Where's Ava?"

"You mean my wife who cryptically made sure I came in for a break at an oddly specific time today?" He looks at me without turning his head. "She's conveniently in the middle of baking something complicated."

I try to think of how to respond to that.

"I know you two have been talking to her. That hasn't been some grand secret," he adds, keeping his tone neutral as I feel the jab.

My brain is swimming with what I've rehearsed but none of it feels right.

Instead of saying anything, I reach into my pocket, past my phone, and grab the box. I know Chase is aware of every movement I make, so I just turn it around in my hands, open it, and set it on the step between us.

The silence stretches for another few moments before he says, "I'm already taken."

Well, I didn't expect him to take it easy on me.

Chapter 59
Avery

I can see why Jackson and Sam didn't work as even a fake couple, but I'm happy he told me to give her a chance. Her overconfident air masks insecurities that most people wouldn't notice.

Now that we're in a quiet setting, and not an auction, I can see how much she fidgets. There are even hand-written notes in the margins or her typed, and very detailed, agenda for our meeting today. According to Tommy, she has these details memorized, so she's over-prepared. Her nails are painted to perfection, matching her flawless outfit, but she picks at them whenever she isn't holding her pen, which she seems to force herself to not fiddle with.

Tommy, on the other hand, is a little bashful whenever Sam makes eye contact with him, but he so obviously has every statistic and point of data ready that's remotely relevant to our conversations. We dive into possible strategies bringing in those who have already shown interest in my co-op approach to Sam's vision for keeping Greenstone a healthy small town instead of slipping into the growing possibility of one that's struggling.

Over the three hours we've been talking, Sam has finally finished one cookie, savoring each bite. I offer her another.

"Oh I couldn't," she says, but I can see her blushing.

"Please," I reply, trying not to push her if she really doesn't want more. "Tommy mentioned that you love peanut butter cookies, so I made them fresh this morning for us. I'm sorry if they're a little uneven, I'm still getting used to Jackson's oven."

She smiles at me. "I was wondering if the rumors were true."

I can feel my eyes go wide, realizing that I haven't really spoken to anyone about living with Jackson the past week other than everyone who messaged and called the day it happened. Tommy said his brothers know and they've stayed at the main house while I'm at mine. But I suppose people talk in a small town.

"Oh," she quickly adds, looking down, "I didn't mean to make it sound like everyone's talking about it or anything, but—"

She cuts herself off, cheeks turning pink and looking down. For some reason, I feel like she's someone who needs to know she didn't overstep.

"No worries. I'm not sure what the rumors are saying, but I've definitely been there quite a bit."

She gives me a look of relief. "He was a lifesaver when I first moved here. Both Jacksy and your brother. I've been meaning to reach out to you."

"I can only imagine how hard it is to be new in such a tight-knit community," I offer.

"Well, Sam has already whipped her whole office into shape, as you can see. I think we have a good shot at getting something sustainable approved once we iron out the rest of the details."

"I have my list of people to reach out to, as well as the four proposed dates for bringing the owners together with the three of us."

"I have my list! Well, I have my list of lists," Sam says, frowning at her notes like she just realized how many she has.

We wrap things up and I send Sam home with the remaining cookies. She only relents when she notes that it wouldn't be polite to decline. I have a feeling she's spent her life trying to please others, but it really seems to fit the little quirks she tries to hide. Maybe the three of us teaming up can help her feel like she really is part of the community.

I stack my binders and tuck them into my tote, say my goodbyes, and then let myself have a moment to breathe on the front porch before going to my truck, letting Tommy keep Sam a little longer. Boots crunch on the gravel as Bryant comes into view around the corner.

I thought they were all going to be working until dinnertime.

Bryant clearly wasn't expecting me, either, because he looks startled when he sees me.

I smile and give him a little wave. He recovers quickly and nods my way and tips his head towards the chairs. I guess we're going to have a chat, then.

Bryant sits down, takes off his black Stetson, and runs a hand through his dark hair and beard. Looking at the hat in his hands, he quietly asks, "You doing okay?"

Maybe because he's the man of few words that it's easy to be fully honest with him. "I hope I will be."

He nods.

"Besides the obvious, are you happy with him?" He looks over at me this time and I hold his gaze, seeing how important it is to him that I'm open.

"I am." I give him a sad, soft smile and I see it reflected on his features.

He stands up and puts one hand on my shoulder.

"It'll work out," he says, giving a little squeeze before letting his hand fall to his side and walking through the door as tears fill my eyes.

One can hope.

Chapter 60
Jackson

"It's for Avery," I say, stating the obvious instead of responding to his joke. "She hasn't opened the box, but she knows it was my grandmother's and she wants this instead of something new."

That gets him to turn and face me, his jaw muscles working overtime.

"How long?"

"Have we been seeing each other?"

He gives one sharp nod.

"It was broached at the auction," I begin.

"Who?"

"That's not–"

"Then it was Avery," he says.

I hold back a sigh because I'm not going to lie again.

"We talked about it in detail on the drive when we moved her back to Greenstone." I don't mention what else happened on that drive since I'd rather not feel his fist connect with my face today.

"We talked about not hurting her that day." His voice can't fully hide the pain and confusion as he absorbs the details.

"I didn't lie to you."

He snorts. "No, I'm sure you chose your words well."

I give him space to say anything else on his mind. This is one of the few times I don't feel confident in reading him.

"Go ahead, I'm sure there's more," he relents.

I hold my hat in one hand and run the other through my short hair, just needing something to do as I start talking. "It's not overly complicated or sinister. We've both had feelings for each other for a long time but didn't know they were reciprocated, and we both tried to get over them. When she came back for the auction, we talked a little on the bus ride about maybe trying things out. On moving day, we made actual plans so we could really test things between us. You know, make sure that we didn't end up driving each other up the wall, and have something stable and proven to not be a fling before telling you so you didn't—"

I just put my own foot right in my mouth.

"Deck you?" Chase offers.

"I walked into that."

Chase snorts.

"But I knew how long I'd been in love with her, which means I know how long I've been lying to my best friend."

"And how long has that been?" he asks before I can continue.

"Remember when Tommy had tickets for the rodeo and he got sick?" I ask.

"That long?"

I shrug. "That's when I figured it out."

He nods.

"So, you lied to me because you hoped to be with her."

"No, I honestly didn't think there was any sort of chance of that. The lie wasn't about not being able to leave her alone. Until she and I established we both wanted more, I was solid in my promise to not date either of your sisters. I lied about only seeing her as a little sister." I avoid saying "baby sister" for once.

Daffodil lays down on Chase's feet and he goes back to picking dirt out of his fingernails as he clears his throat. "Why didn't you ever say anything?"

"It was the one thing you asked of me. And when I first agreed, I thought my feelings were more like a brother/protector. So it was easy to agree."

He tips his head towards the box. "And you already declared your intentions?"

I swallow.

"I didn't last more than a few days before I told her I was in love with her." Chase meets my gaze, searching. "And the night before *this*," I gesture to my face, "I made sure she didn't have any doubts about what I wanted with her."

Chase is quiet and looks straight ahead.

"When we were moving her back to Greenstone, she mentioned testing the waters and I told her that I was diving right in. Lord knows I've tried to connect with other people, but she's it for me. I don't want you to think that we chose each other over you. I can't tell you how to feel or what to think. And I won't try to. I just wanted to make sure that you had a chance to hear from me that this fucking mess of how you found out was us trying to respect you enough by quietly being together to show you that it wasn't a fling. After all these years of me fucking around with other people–"

"You've been clear with them what you have to offer and what you don't," he interjects, startling me.

"I suppose no one could ever accuse me of giving them false hope." Feeling a little lighter and encouraged, I continue. "But my dating history spoke for itself. I've never given you any reason to think it was just some messed up part of me that wouldn't change."

"I assumed it had to do with your mom, honestly."

Surprise washes over me. I know that the way she moved on left a hole, but it somehow didn't occur to me that my dating style evolved from her leaving.

"That's fair."

Another pause settles between us.

"But it was Avery." It's a statement.

"It's always been Avery," I amend.

Chase nods and looks down at his hands that hang loosely between his knees. "Before I ask my only question, and yes, there's only one, I have a few things to say. I'm still sore that you didn't say anything. I guess I get it, but it's going to be a bit before I'm really calm. But, as Ava reminds me almost hourly, it's about damn time I apologize for losing my shit and hitting you. My brain registered what was happening and it screamed that her heart was going to be broken and I'd lose you. Then, I'd quickly grow to resent her and lose her, too. I'm sorry for not giving you two the chance to talk to me and I'm really sorry I fucking hit you. That was way out of line. You're my brother and you're not Jerry."

"No. I deserved getting punched simply because of how you found out."

"It was a little traumatizing."

"I can imagine."

He lets out a breath. "I assume you two haven't tried to kill each other this past week, then."

I shake my head. "Nope."

The silence settles around us. We both stare straight ahead and every now and then Chase wipes his eyes or bobs his head as if he's working through something.

"Okay, then," he says, turning his body to face me. "When do I get to officially make you my brother-in-law?"

Relief pours through me and I scoot over, pulling my best friend into a hug, knocking his hat off his head in the process. When we separate, he looks at me and asks, "So?"

"I might need your help with something before that can happen."

"Name it."

Chapter 61
Avery

My phone vibrates as I'm putting my truck in the garage. I'm trying to stop calling everything "Jackson's" even in my head. He's been so clear that everything is just ours and I like that.

Jackson: Tommy said today went well, I knew it would. Can you leave the folder with the stud info by the computer and file the lineage one away? I'll be home in an hour after I finish up in the stables.

I smile at my organized boyfriend's need to have things a certain way. He's not as particular as Tommy, but he does like having a system in place. I like the message, grab my tote, and head up to the house. I look for Felix in his favorite sunning spot when I come in, but he must have napped near a different window today.

After putting my boots away and dropping my keys in the bowl, I head upstairs to drop off the files and I hear Felix land on the floor and meow his greeting for me. It sounds like he's in the office. Huh, he must have pushed the door all the way open when he came in earlier because we usually leave it ajar.

I walk right in and stop.

Chase is sitting in Jackson's chair.

But Jackson's chair isn't in the right place and neither is his computer. My brain tries to reconcile how my brother is here, but instead, my eyes look to his left and I see that my desk is there. The beautiful desk that he made for me.

My chair is tucked in, my computer stand is there, and everything he prepped for me has been laid out with the exception of the binders that are in my tote right now.

As if Chase senses my current state of confusion, he nods to the wall behind me and I turn around to see the map. Right where Jackson thought it would fit. It's perfect.

After a moment of looking at the map, I turn around completely, my eyes searching Chase's face as I shake my head in disbelief.

"What are you…" I trail off, not sure if I meant to ask what he's doing in this room, why he didn't announce his presence when I came in the house, or why he's here at Jackson's house suddenly after zero communication.

"Doing here?" he supplies for me. "I thought at least part of that answer would have been pretty obvious."

He gestures in the general direction of my desk and my map. Things start to fall into place as my brain catches up.

"You two talked."

He nods. "Jackson stopped by and told me about what has been going on between you two since you moved back. I won't pretend that I wasn't hurt."

Chase rubs his palms together and watches them, which is likely significantly safer to look at considering how our last in-person conversation went down.

"But," he continues, "I do see why you both felt like testing things out in secret so I didn't shit all over it by being an overbearing ass."

He holds up a hand, knowing that I was about to protest him calling himself an "overbearing ass" because if you say something enough times, you'll think it's true. "I really did act like a dick for the past...however many years. You both know why and it's unnecessary to dive into that."

He pauses, clearly taking a moment to find his next words. I don't think Chase has ever been this vulnerable with me in his life, so I give him space to think. He turns his left hand over and watches his ring as he flattens and fists his hand and gives an almost-imperceptible nod while blinking hard a few times.

"I've been a jackass. I shouldn't have painted Jackson into a corner of never being able to love anyone. I don't know how I was such an idiot to have missed the signs that it wasn't about his mom leaving them. He did a damn good job hiding his feelings for you from me so I didn't get more paranoid about losing him and resenting you. But all of that was fear on my part and I fully own up to it." Chase looks right up at me and my tear-filled eyes. "I'm sorry, Avery."

His voice is tight and his face scrunches up. I know he's trying to not cry, but he stands up. "Can you forgive me?"

We've never been in this position before, and I honestly can't tell if he's expecting me to hit him or hug him. I go right in for a hug.

"Obviously," I squeak out as he squeezes most of the air from my lungs. He lets out a shuddering breath and we stand there for a minute with Felix rubbing against our legs.

He relaxes his hold on me and stands up straight. "I brought you something."

"No kidding," I deadpan, sweeping one hand around me at all the things they did while I was at the meeting.

Chase rolls his eyes. "Something Jax doesn't know about. Go look on your chair."

I frown at him as I make my way over to my chair and reach my hand out to pull it away from the desk.

"Gently!" he warns.

"You couldn't put it somewhere that I can't fling it off while finding it?" I mumble, which earns me a chuckle from Chase.

I gently tug the chair back. Sitting on the seat is a gold circle. I look back at Chase with a question on the tip of my tongue.

"It was Grandpa Barnett's," he explains.

My eyes dart back and I pick up the band. It's a simple, no-frills ring that has a good heft to it and slightly rounded edges. It shows signs of being well-worn but looks stronger for it.

"Jax doesn't know that I brought it with me, but if you two want it for him, it's yours. Well, his. But if you don't, that's fine. He brought his grandmother's ring when we talked, and I realized this seemed like a good match when I saw it."

"I haven't looked at it, yet."

"Your ring?"

"No. I wanted things to be right again before I saw it."

I wait, wanting to read his reaction.

"Does that mean you're ready to look now?" he asks, a worried look on his face. He could never hide his emotions.

"Yeah, I think so."

"I think Jackson still has it in his pocket," he says, tipping his head towards the stairs and giving me a cautious smile.

"Thank you," I tell him. "And I'm sorry."

He waves his hand to brush my apology away. "I understand. Ava and I might have had one or two conversations about why you two felt you needed to hide and test things out."

"She's a great woman."

"She'd have to be, to put up with me." He pauses. "How about you walk me to my truck? We left it by Misty's barn so you didn't see it when you got home. I have a feeling you might want to see someone who happens to be killing time doing manual labor over there right now."

My heart gives a happy squeeze to hear Chase call this my home.

Chapter 62
Jackson

Nothing says you're stalling to make sure your best friend and your girlfriend have time to work things out than literally shoveling shit. Especially when you already pay people to do it.

Yet, here I am, going through each stall because I told Chet to take the rest of the day off so I can pile hay that the horses soiled into a wheelbarrow myself.

Most people would have probably cleaned the saddles a second time. Or third. But there's something about the physical labor that helps ease my nerves.

I finish the last stall, throw the rake on top of the pile, and take the wheelbarrow outside to the composting system we have set up for the smaller stable. Once I dump it all in, I grab the nearby hose to rinse off the rake and wheelbarrow, head back inside, and put everything away before cleaning myself up in the sink.

I'm trying to decide what to keep busy with next when I hear the sound of boots crunching on the gravel outside. Muted voices and the sound of Chase's truck starting and driving off follow. Running my hands over my face to make sure I don't have dirt, or worse, on it, I make my way to the entrance.

A short, curvy shadow appears and I can tell Avery put on a sundress today by the silhouette it creates. I pause. My anxiety about going to Chase without her spikes.

She comes into view and I can tell, immediately, that she's been crying. But when she sees me, she breaks into a run and most of my worries wash away.

In a few strides, she's jumping into my arms and wrapping her legs around my waist, crossing her ankles behind my back. Her lips crush mine before I can say anything. I weave one hand into her hair while the other holds her hip.

I couldn't move my head if I tried, her arms somehow have me in a headlock as she presses herself against me. Her tongue commands its way into my mouth and she seeks mine against and again. Something feels different. It's not the same heat as usual, although there's plenty in this kiss. But it feels...unrestrained.

Each time I start to pull back, she immediately closes the fraction of space I create, and I'm sucked back into a kiss that I'd never want to end, if it weren't for that little voice in my head that's wondering if, even though she seem happy, she might be upset that I went to Chase without telling her.

I'm fully aware of how ridiculous that sounds, even in my own head, but we've been through too much already.

Untangling my hand from her hair and bringing it to her face, I cup her cheek in my hand. I slow our kisses to a less frantic, less bruising, pace, feeling our chests press together with each breath.

I search her eyes, trying to get a hint at the cause of her tears, but she closes them and rests her forehead against mine. She sighs in contentment.

"I love you, Jackson."

"I love you, Avery."

She nuzzles her face into my neck, letting her arms drape over my shoulders.

"Thank you," she whispers.

"You never have to thank me, baby."

She nods against me and places a single kiss on my neck.

If I didn't know her, I might think she was trying to test my restraint.

"Did you two get to talk?"

"Yeah." She lifts her head so she's looking right at me. "We did. He knew that I already understood why he was pissed, but it sounds like someone already explained our journey to him earlier today."

"Someone did," I reply.

"Jackson, why are you frowning?"

"Because it seems like you're happy with the outcome, but I'm worried you feel like I went behind your back going to Chase alone," I blurt.

She cocks her head to the side. "No, I don't feel like that, babe."

Relief washes away my anxiety.

"So things are fine between you and Chase?" I ask.

"Of course. I mean, I'm still pissed that he hit you. But he apologized and we talked."

"Good," I say, kissing her forehead.

Somehow, she pulls herself closer against me while keeping her face far enough back so she can take in my expression. Her hands hold my face in place so I can't look anywhere else. Not that I'd ever want to.

She leans back some more and I adjust my hold on her. She's twisting her right hand around her left thumb and is watching it, taking a deep breath.

"Jackson, I just want to be clear about how I feel and where I'm at." She locks her gaze with mine, her green eyes sparkling. "I'm happy to help pick out something for you, or to let you pick out your own, you're a big boy and can handle it if you want to... but, if you'd like, you can wear this one."

She stops fidgeting and pulls a gold band off her thumb and drops it into her palm.

"It was our grandfather's, my dad's dad, who was a really nice man. Actually, you knew him, so I'm clearly babbling." She takes a steadying breath. "But if you'd like for this to be your wedding ring, it's yours."

"Are you serious?" I don't know why that question popped out of my mouth. It's probably the last of my nerves.

She nods her head and says, "Of course."

"Absolutely."

Her entire face lights up with her smile.

"Is it fair that I've seen my ring and you haven't seen yours?" I ask. "Unless you snuck a peek one day."

"I didn't, but I think it would only be fair for me to see it now."

She lets out a squeak as I shift her over to one hip so I can reach into my front pocket to pull out the box.

"Chase said you might still have it on you," she says playfully.

"Can't shovel manure without it," I reply.

"That's what you've been doing and it's been in your pocket?"

"I plead the fifth."

She glares at me with no malice behind it. Her expression immediately shifts as I flip the box open with one hand. She lets out a little gasp as she takes in the gold band set with a simple square-cut diamond surrounded by tiny emeralds.

"It's perfect," she says.

"Then it's good enough to be on your hand."

Chapter 63
Avery

One *month later.*

Jackson swats my hand away for the tenth time. "They're going to be here any minute and they'll appreciate us not constantly sampling the chicken being served."

"I could be doing quality control testing," I reason.

"With Jesse's honey barbecue chicken? He's never made a bad batch."

"You never know."

"Yes, I do. It's fine and we've both sampled plenty."

"It's a good thing you brought home extras or our guests would leave hungry."

"I would never under-order, baby."

Oh boy. Why is that sexy? He's literally telling me that he picks up extra chicken when we have guests over so we can sneak a bunch ahead of time and that just makes me want to drag him upstairs and have my way with him. "Drag" might be an exaggeration because he's more than willing to find an excuse to head upstairs. Well, let's be perfectly honest because location doesn't matter when this man gets the green light...and I give it to him often.

The sound of the first truck pulling up brings me right back to reality. Jackson's face is pure contentment upon hearing it and I know the feeling. The strain of how Chase originally found out has taken a while to fully disappear. You don't forget something like that overnight.

But tonight is the first time we're having our families over. To our place. It's funny that me moving out never occurred to me until my parents asked a few days after Chase and I made up. The conversation was on speakerphone when they happened to ask if I was moving back home soon and Jackson went totally still. It was easier than I ever would have imagined to tell them that I was already home. And Jackson definitely showed his appreciation the moment I hung up.

We head out to the porch together, Jackson's arm instinctively going around my waist with his thumb rubbing my tattoo. Chase practically sprints around the front of the truck to meet Ava, who says she can get out just fine but takes his hand as usual. She's wearing one of her favorite t-shirts which accentuates her bump. My parents let themselves out of the backseat of the cab, watching Chase with knowing smiles.

"You look radiant, Ava!" I tell her as they come up the steps.

"I could say the same to you," she says. "Not that you're pregnant."

Chase looks scandalized at the mere thought, his eyes going wide.

"No, definitely not," I reassure his buzzing mind.

Jackson just gives my hip an extra squeeze as Bryant's truck comes down the driveway with Chuck in the passenger seat, clearly in charge of the music because a high-energy dance mix is blasting out the open windows. Bryant practically skids to a stop, throws the truck in park, and launches himself out of the cab, leaving Tommy and Matt laughing hysterically in the back seat and Chuck looking smug.

Opening the door, Tommy yells, "Courtney's on her way. Her final client went long."

"Lovely to see you, too!" I call back to him, earning an eye roll.

Matt carries a huge pan from the truck and goes right to the oven to warm up the veggies from my family that he prepared for tonight.

"You got it!" Ava squeals as we walk inside.

"You doubted your favorite sister-in-law?"

"I thought Jesse was out of town, so I assumed we'd be having honey roasted chicken on the barbecue and not his honey barbecue chicken." She takes a deep inhale. "This is heavenly. This will be the first time I've had it since Baby Barnett was on the way."

Chase walks up behind her and wraps his arms around her belly, his hands resting on that little bump.

Before I know it, ten minutes have passed and Courtney arrives right when Matt declares the vegetables to be perfect, and we all sit down at Jackson's massive table. We added a bench for one side just for times like this where we can be with everyone we love.

Jackson is completely open with his affection for me and it feels like we've been able to turn his house into the home he hoped it could one day be. Courtney and Chuck crack jokes, even managing to get Bryant to chuckle a few times. My parents admire the photos that are now up around the house, especially the one of all five Landen brothers and their father. Chase sneaks extra chicken onto Ava's plate, much to her delight. Tommy and Matt bring out dessert when it's time, and Jackson holds my hand every chance he gets.

We get to hear Matt talk about bringing Caleb by to ride a stallion Bryant thinks could really do well in the circuits and Tommy's update from Sam on our now-joint co-op because they had lunch today. He only blushes a little when talking about her. Chuck promises to take Ava for another ride in the chopper because she loved the last two so much, making Chase smile. My parents talk Courtney into finally cutting my mom's hair, something she has politely declined out of sheer terror that she'd somehow mess up her best friend's mother's hair. As if she could ever do that.

And Jackson talks about *our* future. No hesitation. No blushing. Just confidence that we're in this together.

I've never had my heart so full.

Chapter 64
Jackson

Eight o'clock comes and goes, and before we know it, half of us are yawning and we're all saying our goodbyes for the night. Avery and I head inside where she puts her glass in the dishwasher and starts turning the plates around since I loaded those earlier.

"About the whole pregnancy thing..." I trail off.

"What about it?" she prods. Of course she's not going to fill in the blanks and make this one easy for me.

"I'm not opposed to it happening in the least, as you know." I pause, not wanting to have this come out the wrong way. "But I'd still like a little more time just the two of us before we start trying."

Fuck, I'm all nerves.

"Babe, are you worried that I'm going to demand you put a bun in my oven after having dinner with a pregnant woman?" Her hand reaches up so she's cupping my face, running her thumb over my cheekbone.

"Well, when you put it that way..." I feel the urge to start babbling.

"We're going to have a family, Jackson. Whether we get pregnant or we adopt. But I need plenty of time to make up for the years we *wanted* to be together," she says, her other hand coming up so she's holding my face, slowly pulling me down to hers. "So if it's okay, I'm not ready to share you just yet."

"Are you thinking you'd like to make up for some of that time now?"

"I'm thinking I'd like to make up for some of that time now."

And then she shifts her hands so they're behind my neck, which is all the warning I need to catch her as she jumps to wrap her legs around me. I make a sound that's a cross between a hum and growl as she kisses my neck, making her way to my ear where she nibbles and flicks the lobe with her tongue as I stride out of the kitchen and straight upstairs, my dick pressing hard against my jeans already.

God, I will always be ready for another round with this woman.

She makes things more challenging as I walk down the hallway when she moves to my mouth, causing a hitch in my step as her tongue immediately demands entrance. Her panting has me ready to sprint the last few steps to our bedroom but having her wrapped around me like this is probably my second-favorite position with her, and I'm about to get her in my most-favorite in a few minutes.

I kick the door the rest of the way open and she releases me with one hand to slam it shut. A few moments later, she's on the bed and my hands roam her body, slipping under her dress to trace her curves and feel her softness. With our mouths fused together, she unbuttons the top of my shirt and heads right for my belt. She knows the exact number of buttons that need to be undone to get my shirts easily over my head and she's wildly efficient now.

Once she pushes my pants and boxer briefs down, she sits up with me, and I pull her dress over her head. My shirt is gone the moment her hands are free again. She grabs my dick, feeling the drops of pre-cum that have gathered already.

"I need you now," she says in desperation.

I shower her neck with kisses.

"Can you be patient so I can have my dessert first?"

She moans the words, "God, yes" as I move down to tease her pebbled nipples with my tongue. She presses her chest up and I work her breast for another minute before kissing my way down her stomach, stopping for a moment on her tattoo.

"Inspect later," she pants, making me chuckle against the horseshoe.

"Your wish is my command."

Instead of taking my time and kissing or licking the rest of the way, I throw one of her thighs onto my shoulder and find her clit with my tongue as I secure her other leg. I shift and drop my knees to the floor, tugging her with me, and then start working her with my fingers. Right when I hit that rough patch and flutter my tongue next to her clit, she gasps, pressing her ass down as her back arches.

"Oh my God, Jackson, more."

If I could tear my mouth away from her fucking pussy for the second it would take me to tell her that I'll always give her more, I would. But that would mean I'd have to slow the progress I'm making towards her first orgasm of the night. Not to mention that I always want to taste her. So when I'm settled between her glorious thighs, I'm like a deep sea diver who isn't coming up until he's found his treasure.

The sounds that come out of her mouth, the way she squirms at times and then grinds down on my face, the view I have of her all make this absolute heaven. I steady the pattern and intensity my tongue is making and I watch the pleasure build.

Her breaths shudder and pause, her eyes flutter closed, her mouth falls open. Her fingers grab the blanket underneath her body, twisting the fabric for a better hold.

And then she throws her head back as she cries out. My fingers keep pumping through the waves of her walls pushing into them. The way her back arches, it looks like her breasts are an offering to an ancient deity.

She slams her back against the bed, changing the angle I have on her clit, but I follow right along to keep the pleasure going. Especially with her legs wrapped so tightly around my face.

Chapter 65
Avery

"Holy shit, I swear you're out to set a record," I say, trying to catch my breath.

Jackson lazily kisses my thighs, letting them fall off his shoulders. He holds up one finger, stands up, and walks over to the jacuzzi, starting the water. As always, the view of his naked form is incredible, sculpted from decades of working the ranch. He turns around and I don't even pretend to be bashful about drinking him in. When he gets back to the bed, he crawls his way up my body until he finally claims my mouth. His hands gently roam my sides and back and it should be calming, but I'm about lose my mind if he's not—

"I can practically hear your thoughts, baby, and even if I couldn't, I'm pretty sure that you're aching for the next round," he murmurs between kisses.

"You're so fucking perfect." He presses against me in all the right places.

"We'll see about that."

The next thing I know, Jackson has pulled some MMA moves and rolled us to the center of our bed so I'm straddling his stomach. He gives me a kiss that sends tingles down my spine and lifts me up.

"Sit back," he instructs, guiding my hips with his hands. As I do, he starts to fill me, inch by glorious inch.

"You have the best ideas," I say through what feels like one long moan until I've taken all of him.

Instead of having me lead, he plants his feet on the bed so he can press his hips up. His hands remain on my hips and keep me suspended when he lowers his, making me feel empty. By now though, I know he can't handle the sensation any longer than I can and he quickly slams himself back into me, continuing to keep me aloft.

Jackson tells me that I must have been made just for him and I believe it. I know he had a very positive review history with his previous partners, so he's good at what he does, but Lord, have mercy, it's like we're a perfect fit with the right amount of stretch every damn time.

This might be my new favorite position, too, with him holding me up, the veins in his arms prominent, and the shake of my body as he slams home. His entire abdomen is flexed to perfection and sweat glistens on his chest and forehead. Every so often his eyes squeeze shut while his mouth parts, which is always followed by a determined look on his face, and I know he's holding off to make sure he doesn't come before me.

Like that'd ever be an issue. He always makes sure he gets me at least twice whenever we're together.

The heat pooling deep inside me shifts into an aching need as he picks up the pace. My fingers curl around his shoulders in an attempt to anchor myself. That small shift changes the angle to something even better and I start pushing back on each thrust to increase the intensity.

I know I'm saying his name over and over, but my brain can't focus on what's coming out of my mouth when my lungs demand a huge inhale and my toes curl. Part of me tries to not dig my nails into Jackson's skin, but I know I'm failing, and Jackson tends to wear any marks from me as a badge of honor.

My thighs tremble and I'm completely consumed with pleasure as my orgasm rips through my body. Jackson always makes sure I don't miss any potential wave as he holds the rhythm steady. I lock my elbows as I finish and hold still while his motions become more frantic. He makes a choked sound before I feel his warmth rush into me. Only when he stops pumping and pulls me against him do I finally let myself collapse, almost slipping right off of him with our sweat-slicked bodies.

We both let out a sigh at the same time and I shift so I can kiss him, slow and sure.

"The tub has to be almost full by now."

His fingers trace feather-light paths up and down my arm. "Eager to leave the bed, are you?"

"No, but I might be eager to have those jets running while I sit in your arms."

"Good assumption that we're both getting in," he says. He sits up, bringing me along for the ride.

He scoops me up, like I weigh nothing at all, and carries me to the jacuzzi. Jackson settles us in with the jets on full blast, his head tipped back and eyes closed. I'm not ashamed of the moan I release at how amazing this feels. We stay this way until our fingers and toes look like prunes, just soaking together, kissing, and holding each other.

I wake up in my favorite place in the world: completely entangled with Jackson. He's rubbing my back with light fingers when I get an idea.

I shift up his body to kiss him. "Give me a minute."

He looks at me, slightly confused. "Okay?"

Tossing on my robe, I hear him call out "Unnecessary!" as I leave the bedroom. I could walk this path in my sleep. I snag the box on the desk and turn right around.

"I meant to grab them after everyone left, but someone distracted me," I tell him, holding the box out.

"Oops, that was my bad," he says with a smirk as I crawl back to him.

I snort. "I wanted us to try them on and to talk about when we want to start wearing them."

"Are you looking to set a date, Avery Barnett?"

"I might be interested in something along those lines."

"How about tomorrow?" he asks, dropping a kiss to my shoulder.

"How about a day that our families might be able to attend?"

"Fair enough," he says. "When is Susan visiting next?"

"In about two months."

"Let's do that."

"Are any of your brothers going to be gone?"

"No, they should be here."

"So we're making this legally binding when she's in town?"

He nuzzles my neck. "Yes please."

I tilt my head to the side to give him better access and he spoils me with kisses. That wakes me up enough that I remember why

I grabbed them in the first place. "What do you think about finally trying them on?"

"I'd say that sounds like an excellent idea."

He holds out his left hand, fingers straightened. I slip my grandfather's ring on like it was made for him. "It looks amazing."

"My turn," he says, opening the box while letting me hold it in place. He pulls out the ring and waits for me to set the box to the side. "Are you ready?"

"I am."

The ring is a perfect fit and worth the wait, just like us.

Acknowledgements

With this being my debut, a lot of people gave advice, feedback, and guidance along the way, and I'm grateful for each and every one of you! There are a few specific thank yous that I need to say:

Andra, Anna, Ashley, and Melissa - your feedback was incredible and helped shape this story into what it is today - thank you!

Baddie - you have been fantastic through this in all the different ways you've been part of this - thank you!

Brandi - you have been wonderful to work with and you understood my vision from the start - thank you!

Evy - my partner in this journey... I'm so happy we're in this together - here's to many more stories!

Sarah - you made my cover and literally walked me through countless things for publishing - a huge thank you!

To my author friends - you have been invaluable. Thank you for being part of a community that uplifts one another!

To my family - a gigantic thank you. It's not every day someone tells you they wrote a book with some smut in it! You've been absolutely incredible!

To every reader who picked this up - thank you from the bottom of my heart

What's next?

Are you ready for Tommy's story? Check it out at http://www.books2read.com/for-sam

Don't miss any releases and freebies:

About the Author

Portrait by Three Ravens Art

Natalie Jess is a Midwest author who loves living in a place with snowy winters. She grew up reading way past her bedtime and never broke that habit - except now the books she reads, and writes, are definitely for adults.

You can find her online at NatalieJessAuthor and www.natalieandevy.com.

www.ingramcontent.com/pod-product-compliance
Lightning Source LLC
Chambersburg PA
CBHW051213190726
48288CB00006B/1940